continued . . .

Also by Laura Wright

The Cavanaugh Brothers Series
Branded
Broken

Mark of the Vampire Series
Eternal Hunger
Eternal Kiss
Eternal Blood
(A Penguin Special)
Eternal Captive
Eternal Beast
Eternal Beauty
(A Penguin Special)
Eternal Demon
Eternal Sin

BRASH

THE CAVANAUGH BROTHERS

Laura Wright

A SIGNET ECLIPSE BOOK

SIGNET ECLIPSE
Published by the Penguin Group
Penguin Group (USA) LLC, 375 Hudson Street,
New York, New York 10014

USA | Canada | UK | Ireland | Australia | New Zealand | India | South Africa | China
penguin.com
A Penguin Random House Company

First published by Signet Eclipse, an imprint of New American Library,
a division of Penguin Group (USA) LLC

First Printing, March 2015

Copyright © Laura Wright, 2015

SIGNET ECLIPSE and logo are trademarks of Penguin Group (USA) LLC.

ISBN 978-0-451-46508-5

Printed in the United States of America
10 9 8 7 6 5 4 3 2 1

Diary of Cassandra Cavanaugh

May 5, 2002

Dear Diary,

I think Sweet's right. Someone is following us. This is what happened. I was at the drugstore today after school. I was hoping maybe Sweet would come in because I haven't seen or heard from him in three days. And it's where we first locked eyes and all. I really wanted to know why he didn't meet me the other night like he said he was going to. I wanted to know if it was because of the kiss. I practiced it on my hand a couple of times, and I didn't think it was all that bad. Well, he did come in. He was buying all sorts of strange things like headache medicine and baking soda. He looked surprised to see me. But when I went up to him, he smiled his amazing smile and told me he'd meet me behind the diner in ten minutes.

Diary, I waited for a half hour, and he didn't come. Why would he do that? Did something happen to him? Does he just not like me anymore?

My brain tells me to hate him, but my heart tells my brain to shut up. Who do I listen to?

Stupid boys.

Okay, here's the weird part. When I was walking over to the diner, I felt someone's eyes on me. I looked all around and didn't see no one. But I swear they were there!

What if it's one of my brothers?

Maybe they discovered what we've been doing!!

I could ask 'em? Or talk to Mac? I'm so confused. I hate how my heart feels right now. Heavy and broken.

Cass

One

Cole Cavanaugh watched as Johnny Blair dropped his needle into the red ink, then resumed his special brand of torture.

"You gonna tell me what this stands for, man?" Johnny asked, working the final curve of a C on Cole's shoulder. "Or do I need to guess?"

Cole smirked at the Austin-based artist who had inked nearly every one of his tats. "Guess away, brother."

Black brows lifted over pale green eyes. "Woman's initials?"

Cole snorted. "Hell, no."

The guy chuckled, the two small studs in his lower lip flattening against his teeth. "Your next victim in the ring?"

"Nah, man. That joker's blood on my knuckles is all the stain I need." He glanced down at the finished artwork. "These three C's are for the ranch where I grew up."

Johnny placed the tat gun on the metal side table beside Cole's chair. "I didn't know you were a ranch boy, Cavanaugh."

"Born and bred."

"And now branded," the man said as he cleaned Cole's skin, then slathered some A&D ointment on it.

"Let's get to bandaging," Cole said, not wanting to go any further into discussions about the Triple C and how he grew up and why he left. Some shit needed to stay private outside River Black. "I have training in an hour."

Johnny shook his head but grabbed the bandages and tape. "Will it do any good if I tell you to wait until tomorrow? Give this some time to heal?"

Tomorrow wouldn't be possible. He was heading back to the ranch tonight. "Thirteen tats and I've never had a problem."

"Fine," Johnny said. "I'm gonna wrap it up extra good, but if someone knocks you there, it's going to hurt like a motherfucker."

"I'm counting on it," Cole said without thinking.

"Damn," Johnny said, fitting the bandage. "Had no idea you were such a masochist."

He wasn't. Not really. Well, maybe in the beginning, right after Cass had been taken, after he'd left home and gone underground. Maybe then he'd wanted to feel the pain. Hell, maybe he'd thought he deserved it. But now it was all about vengeance. Every fight. Every bruise. Every drop of blood. It belonged to the one who got away . . . with murder.

He eyed the tattoo artist. "Just makes my adrenaline rush. Heightens my awareness. Fuels the fight. That kind of thing."

"When's your match?" Johnny asked him.

"Next week."

"Who you beatin' down?"

"Fred Fontana."

The man's head jerked up fast. "Oh, shit."

Oh, shit's right, Cole thought with a dry grin. Fred Omega Fontana had a rep for nearly killing anyone who stepped into the ring with him. He was the one bastard Cole had yet to beat. The ungettable get. The ultimate in vengeance.

"You ready?" Johnny asked as he pushed back in his chair and stripped off his gloves. "Physically? Mentally? All that shit?"

"Hell, yeah," Cole told him.

But the words were forced. So was the hard-ass show he was putting on. The fire and fury that normally pulsed in his blood this close to a fight weren't there. Maybe too much had happened lately. Marriages and engagements. Inheriting the Triple C along with his brothers. Including a brother he never knew he had. And too many damn memories assaulting him at every turn. It was why he'd decided to get the Triple C brand inked into his skin. He was hoping it would put that wicked heat, that anger, that venom he'd felt when he'd run from the place back into his gut and heart. Because, fuck him, if it didn't show up and do its job in the ring next week, the hope of finding out the truth about his sister's death wasn't the only thing he was going to lose. He might very well lose his life.

"You have issues, Belle," Grace Hunter told her passenger, an aging basset hound who had just howled her damn head off as they drove past the Triple C ranch.

And it wasn't the first time.

Any time Belle got within spitting distance of where Cole Cavanaugh hung his hat, the dog howled.

Grace glanced over at the pup, sitting on her cute rump, buckled in, head out the open window of Grace's blue 1960 Dodge pickup, long ears flapping in the breeze. "He's not interested in you, Miss Girl. He was only out for information."

Belle ignored the reminder that Cole Cavanaugh's visit to the vet clinic a few days ago— under the pretense that he wanted to adopt the basset hound—was a lie. As soon as Grace had slipped out of the office, that rat bastard had gone through her files and found out where her ill and aging father was living.

"He hasn't been back in days," she reminded Belle as she got onto the highway. "Probably off practicing for that bloodbath he calls a job." She grimaced at the thought. She'd never actually been to a fight, but she imagined it was horrific. "You don't want that kind of guy buying your kibble, now do you?"

This time Belle turned to look at her. Droopy eyes and a glorious frown.

"Someone who beats people up for a living?" Grace asked.

The basset hound barked.

"Yeah, yeah, I know he's good-looking and un-predictable, and charming in an overbearing way," Grace continued, "but let me tell you from experience: that combination is nothing but trouble. Those kinds of guys are all *Love 'em and leave 'em*. Or in my case, *Screw 'em and take off in the middle of the night*." Grace exhaled heavily as she recalled the majority of her college dating experiences.

Belle seemed unconvinced, and once again turned to stare out the window.

"Fine. Don't say I didn't warn you. But when he breaks your heart, don't come crying to me."

For exactly thirty seconds, she held on to that threat. Then she caved. Oh, who was she kidding? Sweet Belle could come crying to her anytime, and Grace would take her in her arms and let her know it was okay. Then, later, when they were sharing a pint of ice cream, she would gently counsel the canine that if she wanted a real future with someone who would be there for her through thick and thin, she needed to look for stable instead of stunning, reliable instead of reactive. And instead of inked-up skin and hard waves of muscles, a balanced, tender, soulful heart.

She pulled off the highway and headed toward the center of town. Speaking of tender hearts, she was going to see her dad today. See if she could get him to clear up this mess with Caleb Palmer. Not only was her father's best friend in jail for assaulting James Cavanaugh's fiancée, he'd claimed to know something about Cass Cavanaugh's abduction and murder. *God, what happened all those years ago?* she thought as she turned into the Barrington Ridge Senior Care parking lot and found a space. And what had happened to Caleb? Except for her time spent in school, Grace had known the man fairly well. She'd never seen a bad side to him. But, clearly, a monster resided within. He'd hurt Sheridan O'Neil, could've killed her, and Grace prayed he'd never get out of jail. Now all she was interested in was clearing her father's name. Making sure everyone knew that he wasn't connected to Caleb's actions and insinuations. Hell, she didn't want him connected to Caleb in any way, if she could help it. No visits, no phone calls. Maybe then she could finally get the Cavanaughs off her back.

Especially the tattooed one.

With Belle leashed and walking beside her, Grace

entered the front door of the care facility and headed down the hall. Gentle piano music played from the overhead speakers and the scent of cleaning products and breakfast foods hung thickly in the air. Barrington Ridge had cleared her request to bring Belle along. Her dad had owned a dog for many years—one that had been at his side or in his patrol car nearly day and night—and Grace was hopeful the canine would stir his memory. Or at the very least keep him calm and lucid while they talked.

"Awww, ain't she sweet?" one of the nurses remarked as they passed by.

"Hiya, Grace," another one called from behind the desk.

"Morning, Elisabeth, Bev," Grace returned cheerfully. She pointed to her father's door. "He awake?"

Phone to her ear, Beverly nodded. "Just finished his breakfast 'bout ten minutes ago."

"Thanks," Grace said, moving down the corridor as Belle tried to sniff every inch of the floor, wall, and desks.

Bright sunlight and the heavy scent of bacon welcomed Grace as she entered the room. As usual, her father was seated at the small table near the window. He liked the light and the breeze, just as he had at home. His nose was in a magazine and he was flipping through the pages at lightning speed. Steam rose from a coffee cup to his right.

"What are we reading today, Dad?" she asked, coming over and slipping into one of the chairs beside him. "Fishing or dirt bike racing?"

Peter Hunter glanced up and smiled brightly when he saw her. At sixty-three, he was still a very handsome man. Had all of his dark hair, and those hazel eyes—when lucid—were sharp and curious. "Gracie?"

Grace's heart ballooned inside her chest and exploded in a rush of gratefulness. It was the way of it now. Every time she walked into his room, she wondered if his eyes would flash with warm recognition or cool disinterest.

"Hi, Dad," she said with gentle warmth, leaning forward. This was the man who had become her everything when her mother had passed from a car accident when she was ten. This was the man who had tucked her into bed at night, made her spaghetti and s'mores, and green smoothies when she was on a health kick. The man who had let her stay up late and told her stories about his adventures as sheriff. Protected her, loved her, treated her like she was the most special thing in the world. Made her believe she could be anything she wanted to be.

Her hero.

She reached for his hand and gave it a squeeze. He squeezed back.

"Who's the mongrel?" he asked good-naturedly.

Grace grinned. "This is Belle. She's a friend of mine."

Her father reached down and gave the basset hound, who had been waiting patiently beside the table, a pat on the head and a rub under the chin. Belle leaned into him and licked his hand. For a moment it seemed as though her father was as content and happy and clear as she'd seen him of late. But after a moment, his face fell and he pulled his hand away. "Those eyes . . . she looks about as miserable as I feel," he ground out bitterly.

Grace pushed back the wall of pain that threatened to steal her hope and faith. "Why are you miserable, Dad?"

"Stuck in here when I have a job to do," he explained, his chin lifting in that way it always did when he talked about his work as a sheriff. "People out there who need me. If I'm not sprung soon, I could lose my job, Gracie. Your mama doesn't bring in enough midwifing."

God, it hurt her so much to hear him talk about the past as though it was the present. Thinking her mom was still alive. But hurt didn't help him, and it sure didn't do anything to protect his good name.

"Dad," she began gently. "I need you to tell me about Mr. Palmer."

His dark brows rose and he looked momentarily interested. "Caleb?"

She nodded.

"Well, honey, he is my very best friend." A hint of a smile played about his lips. "Good man. Right good man. Always there for me. That's how friends should be. Don't you forget that."

Grace reached down and started stroking Belle's head. "He's done something terrible."

Her father didn't even hesitate before answering. "No, no, baby. Not him."

"Yes, Dad," she insisted, breath caught in her lungs, bracing herself for what was coming. "He hurt a woman."

"What do you mean, hurt?" He sat back in his chair looking utterly dumbstruck for a moment. Then his skin went cow udder white and he gasped. "Lord Almighty! He takin' the blame for that, is he?"

Shit. So her father had already heard about the attack. Grace would have to speak to Bev and Elisabeth. In his condition, he shouldn't be hearing about such upsetting things from anyone but her.

"He admitted it, Dad. There were witnesses and a police report. And the woman's going to testify against him."

A sad smile touched Peter Hunter's mouth. "How can she, baby? She's dead."

A boulder the size of Texas rolled through Grace and sat there, festering in her belly. Her pulse pounded savagely in her blood. Instead of asking him to clarify his words or continue, she wanted, more than anything, to get up and walk out. But she had to ask, didn't she? It's why she'd come. To find out what he knew. To find out the truth.

"Who are you talking about, Dad?" she began softly.

"That girl, Gracie dear." His gaze shifted to his magazine and he started thumbing through the pages once again. "Cass Cavanaugh."

Two

"You two should be on an island somewhere," Cole grumbled, dropping into a chair. "Those looks you're passing between you gotta be making everyone in this place damn uncomfortable."

"What looks?" Sheridan asked, turning away from her fiancé to stare confusedly into the faces of her new family, who were all clustered around a table inside the decently packed Bull's Eye.

Cole just snorted. Love. It made his lip curl. The idea of it. The weakness of it. Could slice you in two, drop you to your knees if you gave in to it. How the hell his brothers had fallen off the face of the earth into that pit of bullshit he'd never know. But he wanted no part of it. Ever.

Leaning in close to Sheridan's ear, Cole's brother James bit the lobe gently. "I think he's referring to how I look when I'm staring at you, honey. Hungry," he added on a growl. "And not for food."

Cole groaned. "Come on. I just got here. Can I at least order something before the two of you make me puke?" He grabbed a menu and ripped it open. He was starving. That's what eight hours a day of training did to a guy.

"Got a bug up your ass, little brother?" Deacon inquired dryly, one brow raised over amused green eyes.

"Because I don't want to bear witness to your mutual descent into the hell of wedded bliss?"

Deacon's lips twitched. "That's cold."

"I'd say so," Mac agreed, her blue eyes sparkling as she slipped her arm through Deacon's.

Of course she'd say so, Cole thought. His sister-in-law, who also happened to be the forewoman of the Triple C, was all happy and agreeable now that she'd married her childhood crush. Forget the fact that her new husband had only a few weeks earlier tried to destroy the one thing she loved above all else. The Triple C.

'Course, Deac wasn't interested in that anymore. *Love*.

He sneered. Changed things for a while maybe. But it wasn't something a person could count on to last. The pain would find you soon enough.

"Don't pay him any mind, y'all," James said, scooping up his beer and taking a swig. "He's one week from a fight."

Tipping back his hat, Deacon's eyes widened with understanding. "Ah, right."

"What?" Sheridan asked, looking from one brother to the next. Deacon's beautiful assistant had been around the brothers for only a short time. She had a lot to learn. Not that she wasn't capable. Filly was damn smart.

"What's the one week about?" she continued.

"Fists Cavanaugh here is just livin' in the world of the deprived, is all," Deacon told her with a grin.

"Poor baby," James added, his ocean-colored eyes flashing with the opposite of sympathy.

Shithead.

Cole ordered a burger with cheese but no bun from the passing waitress, then turned back to his family—the ones who had called his ass home tonight. "First of all, go to hell. Second, let me know when y'all are done chappin' my ass, 'K?"

Mac looked utterly nonplussed as she popped a French fry in her mouth. "Someone better clue me in here. Was/is Cole poor and/or deprived?"

Sheridan, who was seated on the other side of her, explained, her business voice cranked up to high, "I believe it might have something to do with the rules fighters follow before a match. The things they abstain from."

"You got it, honey," James said, dropping a kiss on her cheek.

"Like what?" Mac asked.

"Oh, come on," James said on a laugh. "You ain't that innocent, are you, Mac?"

She reached past Sheridan to punch him in the arm. "Shut up."

James chuckled. "Your woman's got some power behind that muscle, Deac."

"Tell me something I don't know," the man returned.

"Alcohol is one, I imagine," Sheridan continued, her tone still edged with boardroom coolness.

Cole groaned. *Christ. Nothing sounds better than a cold beer right now.*

"And sex is probably another."

Except that.

Fuck.

"Is it sex or alcohol, Cole?" Deacon asked, then drained the rest of his beer.

"Kill me now." Cole grunted.

"No can do. Fontana wants that chance," James said. "So just keep the faith and—"

"Keep your fly zipped?" Mac tossed out in a questioning voice, grinning like a cat.

The table erupted into laughter.

"Is this the reason you guys wanted me back here tonight?" Cole demanded peevishly. "To jerk my chain fifty ways to Sunday?"

The question quickly blanketed the laughter. Eyes dropped to drinks and the tabletop. Of course that wasn't the reason they'd asked him to come home, and Cole knew it. He took a swig of his ice water. Wished it was tequila.

"Palmer." Deacon said the word in an almost menacing voice.

Teeth tightly clenched, Cole uttered, "You able to get in to see him?"

"Yep."

Cole's gaze came up, narrowed. "Shit. And?"

The man's once amused expression was now stone cold. "I got in, but he refuses to see me."

Cole rapped the table. "Goddammit, Deac. With all your money and connections you couldn't get that done."

"His rights supersede my influence."

"Rights," Cole ground out. "That piece of shit shouldn't have rights. He knows the truth about Cass."

"That's what he claimed," James said quietly.

What was this? Cole stared at the blue-eyed horse whisperer who had found love like some people find God. "You don't believe it now?"

The man shrugged. "I had him in a chokehold at Deac and Mac's wedding, for Christ's sake. I was amped up, ready to take him out—"

"Should've done it," Cole ground out.

"My point is, he could've said he knew who killed Cass just to get my hands off his neck. Could've been a bluff."

"Bullshit." Cole couldn't believe his brothers were thinking this way. "He knows something—and so does his best friend, Sheriff Hunter."

Deacon dropped an arm across Mac's shoulders

and sighed. "It's possible. But we can't get to either of them. Because of you and James and that unwelcome visit to Hunter's care facility, there's a restraining order out against us. And Palmer's wife and daughter are no longer working at the bakery. The place is closed indefinitely."

"What?" Cole hadn't heard that.

"Couldn't take the scandal," Mac told him. "All the questions. A couple of reporters came down from Dallas. Palmers ain't sophisticated people. It was too much."

As the waitress placed the burger before him, a sinking feeling started to move through Cole. What the hell was going on here? He'd been away for a few days training, and he'd come back to roadblocks and no plan. They had to get to Palmer, find out what he knew—what he believed.

"Sure, there are lots of *maybe*s and *possibly*s going around here, but that doesn't mean we don't check out every lead we got." His eyes shifted between the two men. "Or maybe things have changed in the past couple of days? Maybe you two are so caught up in your new and shiny lives, you want to put our sister on the back burner." He sneered at his brothers. "That what happens when you're getting laid regularly? Your brain shrinks and your balls disappear?"

"Hey!" Mac called out.

"Don't go there, little brother," Deacon began, his tone a low, clear warning.

"You know damn well we want the truth," James added.

Cole laughed at them all. It was a bitter, ugly sound, and he didn't much care for it.

Mac was staring at him hard.

"What?" he demanded.

"You think I don't want to know the truth about my best friend?"

Her voice was clear and true, but the flash of pain-laced defiance made Cole falter. Made him wonder if he'd gone too far. Seems he was doing that quite a bit lately.

Deacon released a weighty breath and played with the empty beer bottle beside his glass. "It's just going to take a different plan of action. A new strategy. And while we're working that out, we need to decide the fate of the Triple C."

"My workplace, let's not forget," Mac added quietly, her eyes still heavy with all the talk of Cass.

Deacon pulled her in close. "No one's forgetting that, darlin'."

"I say, give it to the Cavanaugh bastard and be done with it," Cole said without heat. He couldn't care less about the C. Not right now anyway. He felt frustrated and mixed up about what was happening—what had been happening over the past month. He wanted the truth about what had happened to Cass, and yet there was a deep, dark place inside him that didn't want to know. Didn't want to face the fact that he hadn't been there for his twin, hadn't protected her from the bastard who'd ripped her from his life . . .

When he glanced up, he found the four of them staring at him.

"I'm serious," he said. "That brother of ours has been livin' here for most of his life. None of us wants the place. Mac'll stay on with him running things."

"We can't be sure of that," Deacon said. "Besides, one of us does want it."

Cole stilled. "Who?"

James looked first at Sheridan, then at Cole. "We do."

We! Good fucking Christ. These women were changing everything. Messing shit up—messing with heads. First Deac was going to destroy the Triple C. Then Mac stepped in, and now he had a new ranch built and was sticking around town. James hadn't given a shit about the Triple, and now with Sheridan wearing his ring, he wanted to stay here in River Black and—what, make it their home? Damn lovebirds. Hadn't they all silently agreed to keep away from this town? This goddamned town that had destroyed them all? They didn't belong here . . . not anymore. At least Cole still believed that.

"The horses . . ." James began. "They need to be looked after."

"So visit them," Cole ground out. His appetite was gone. "You don't have to live there."

"Don't have to, true," James agreed with a nod.

"But I think I want to. *We* want to. Split time between here and Dallas, like Deac does."

Heat vibrated through Cole's body. He looked at James, then Deacon. "I feel like I don't even know the two of you anymore."

"You're overreacting," Deacon began.

Cole's phone vibrated and he glanced down at the readout. His jaw clenched as his eyes moved over the name. Jesus, the day was just getting better and better. What did she want? To tell him that she was coming into town tonight and he'd better stay thirty feet away from her at all times?

> This is Grace Hunter. I don't know if you're in River Black, but I'd like to meet w/you ASAP.

The vet's face popped into his mind. She had a real pretty face. The kind a man could stare at for hours and not get bored. Too bad she was a giant pain in the ass. He typed.

> *I'm in RB.*

What was this? he wondered. Contacted by Grace Hunter out of the blue. The woman had wanted him nowhere near her after his little breaking and entering at her office, followed up by the visit to her dad. And then there was that little matter of the restraining order out on him. He couldn't afford trouble a week before his fight. And how had she gotten his private cell number?

Can you meet me @ 10 Ruddyfern Drive. 30 mins?

What's on Ruddyfern?

My house.

One of Cole's eyebrows jerked up. This had to be a prank. He snorted.

Will there be law enforcement waiting for me?

No

Handcuffs?

Shit, he couldn't help himself with that one. There was a second or two before she responded. Then . . .

I can't tell if you're being funny or a jackass.

How 'bout both? Just don't wanna be arrested tonight, darlin.

I've dropped the restraining order.

Surprise roared through him. What the hell? Why would she do that? Really, was this a prank? Payback for what he'd done? *Go and ask her, dumbass.* He stared at the text. From what he'd learned about Grace Hunter, she didn't play around. She was tough and serious and rigid—not to mention hardcore about protecting her dad from the big bad Cavanaugh brothers. He frowned.

"You still with us, little brother?" James said, yanking Cole out of his reverie.

Whatever it was the vet wanted from him, Cole was too damn curious—not to mention opportunistic—to ignore it. He pushed back his chair and stood up. "I gotta go."

"Wait—what?" Deacon sat back, arm still wrapped protectively around Mac's shoulder. "We need to talk about this. Make a plan of action. Get things settled with the Triple C."

Cole didn't answer Deac. He was making a plan of action, and if it turned out to be something of use, he'd let his brothers in on it. He eyed James. "You want the Triple C? Take my part, take Deac's part, and there you go. Done. Bastard Boy is out on his ass."

"Jesus," James uttered. "You're really out of your mind tonight."

Cole didn't answer. Just turned and walked away. He was keyed up, wanted to know what awaited him on the other end of that text.

"Hey," James called after him.

"Let him go," Deacon said. "He's not going to be rational until the fight's over."

Passing by a few rowdy tables, Cole headed for the door. He wondered if what Deacon said was true. Or if sensible thinking was completely gone from him now, leaving only reactionary asshole. Either way, Dr. Grace Hunter had just opened the door to whatever he was at this moment and he was about to walk on in.

Crouched in the bushes at the side of the house, Grace Hunter watched the small shadow creep across the lawn toward her. *Oh yeah, it's over, buddy. This war between you and me.*

As if hearing her silent promise, the figure stopped, a bottlebrush tail shooting straight up in the air. Grace held her breath. *Don't you dare turn around.* She had to get him this time. Make sure he didn't cause any more trouble. Make sure he didn't make any more babies. If only he'd be reasonable. But cats rarely were. Especially the toms. The males. Nothing could ever be simple and straightforward. One always had to connive and plot and threaten and convince.

And even then, sometimes they don't return your texts.

Who are we talking about now, Grace? she chided herself. Cats or Cole Cavanaugh? It had taken every ounce of both her pride and her good sense to text Cole Knock-Out Cavanaugh and ask him to come by to talk with her. The guy was 190 pounds (she was guessing, of course) of gorgeous, hard-muscled, tatted-up trouble. But she knew he and his brothers weren't going to stop looking for answers about their sister. Looking for answers in her father's direction.

She sighed. She'd wanted to believe he had none. But after their back-and-forth today, it seemed her father might have something locked away in his receding brain.

The shadow, straight tail and all, turned in a slow circle, contemplating its next move.

Oh, Dad, she thought with deep sadness. Her dear, sweet, amazing father, who had taken on the role of both parents, pushed her to follow her dreams of working with animals—even when her grades had started slipping after the accident. When she'd barely wanted to get out of bed in the morning. He'd been her biggest supporter, her champion—even her shoulder to cry on when one charming college loser after another had broken her heart.

He knows something about Cass Cavanaugh's murder.

Her heart bled at the thought, at the realization. She'd gone over and over what he'd said this morning. What he'd implied. She knew in her gut her father hadn't hurt the Cavanaugh girl, but maybe . . . *Oh God, could he have helped Palmer cover it up?* Disappointment swirled inside her. How could he? Why would he? Because of friendship? Or had Palmer threatened him? So many questions she wanted answered. But one thing was sure: she wasn't about to let him go to jail. Christ, he was already in a jail of sorts. She had to protect him, clear his name. She wasn't altogether sure that teaming up with Cole Cavanaugh was the answer. In fact, it could be a complete nightmare. But she wanted to know what the fighter knew, wanted to keep him close as he gained information—maybe even lead him off track if fingers started to point in the direction of her father.

The cat was weaving in and out of the hydrangeas now. Making his way toward the steps. Grace's breath caught in her throat. So close. If she could just lean in another—

Suddenly, the bottlebrush tail disappeared as large, skilled, tattooed hands scooped him up as if he were nothing fiercer than a stuffed animal.

"Lose something, Doc?" came the throaty sound of Cole Cavanaugh's voice.

Grace's heart stuttered inside her chest as she looked up. Where the hell had he come from? Her head swiveled right, took in the truck at the curb and the open gate. How hadn't she heard him drive up? Park? Open and close his door? Had she been that lost in thought?

She glanced back to him. Dressed in blue jeans, polished black cowboy boots, and a white T-shirt, Cole Cavanaugh was every bit as tall, imposing, and fiercely rugged as his brothers—with one stunning difference: thickly muscled arms covered in vibrant ink. Grace's eyes moved down one of those arms to the huge black-and-orange tom tucked into the man's side.

"How did you do that?" she asked, finding her voice. She wasn't sure where it had disappeared to while she was staring at his forearm and the incredible artwork rendered there—a snake with a skull for a face.

"Do what?" he asked.

Realizing she was still in a crouched position, she quickly stood and gestured to the tom.

He snorted. "Pick up a little kitty cat?"

She bristled at his arrogance. If she was admitting the truth—only to herself, of course—Cole Cavanaugh was one of the sexiest men she'd ever met. But his overconfidence brought her right back to college. To those boys she'd found irresistible. No more. Not ever again. She was all about stable now. And nice, and part of the community. Like Reverend McCarron. Wayne.

She needed to remember that. Just Wayne.

"I've been trying to catch him for two weeks," she informed Cole, brushing dirt from her jeans.

"That sucks," he said before opening his arms and letting the cat go.

Momentarily stunned, Grace watched the tom drop to his paws. "Wait— Don't—" Then it took off down the path. "Dammit!" She pushed past Cole and ran after it. When she reached the bottom of the driveway, she stopped and stared out into the blackness. Unbelievable. She scrubbed a hand over her face. He was gone. Shocked and pissed, she whirled around. "Why the hell did you do that?" she yelled. "What is your problem, Cavanaugh?"

Cole looked baffled. "He wanted out of my arms."

"I don't give a shit!"

"He wanted out of here."

"He needed to be caught."

"Says you." One pale eyebrow jerked up. "Not everything is meant to be caught, Doc."

She stared back, shaking her head. *So arrogant.* She didn't know what Belle saw in him. "That's you talking. About yourself."

"An animal's an animal, honey."

Honey?!? "This is a stray, Cole."

He just stared at her. Unfazed, uninterested.

"He needed to be fixed," she continued.

A slow grin moved over his face. Grace might've found it debilitatingly sexy if she wasn't ready to knock the guy over the head with a tree branch.

"Guys gotta look out for each other," he said with a shrug.

That was it. Fuming, she stalked toward him. Didn't stop until she was a couple of inches from his face. "You think this is funny, Cavanaugh?"

The smile remained as he stared down at her. He was all sharp angles and full lips, and his eyes were disquieting. They were the color of obsidian. She'd never seen that color on a human. Cats, sure. But not on a human. His nostrils flared as if taking in her scent. She wondered what he caught. Peach shampoo with a side of hard-core vitriol?

"Do you have any idea how many homeless kittens you just helped create?" she said through tightly gritted teeth.

His expression changed in an instant. From casual to wary. "No."

"'Course not. And those kittens are liable to starve, or be eaten by a coyote, or hit by a truck. Or unceremoniously euthanized, if they ever even make it to a shelter, which are in short supply around here."

He pulled in a sharp breath, and for the first time Grace saw a thread of understanding cross his features. Or was it regret? Hell, at this point, she'd take either one.

"Look, I'm sorry, okay?" he said. "I'll help you find him."

She shook her head, feeling dispirited. "He's long gone."

"Well, we can try. It's something."

"Please don't pretend you care."

"I'm not pretending."

She looked up at him into those onyx eyes, trying to see the forest for the trees, as her dad used to say. But all she got was a wall.

His nostrils flared. "Maybe you should tell me why I'm here, Grace."

Yeah, maybe.

They were close. Too close. It was making her a little dizzy. And a little stupid. If he leaned down, even an inch or two. And if she arched up on her toes a little . . .

Yes. Definitely stupid.

She stepped back. "Why don't you come inside." God, she hated how breathy her voice sounded. Breathy girls didn't make good decisions. Probably because oxygen wasn't getting to their brains.

His brows lowered. "What's inside?" he asked suspiciously.

"Just want to talk to you."

"We can do that out here."

"Jeez. Are you afraid of me or something?"

"Kind of," he admitted wryly. "You sure that restraining order's been dropped?"

A touch of a smile curved her lips. "Yes. I took care of it this afternoon." She turned and headed for the porch steps. "But, you know, if you don't trust me, you can always use my phone to call and check."

"I got my own phone, thanks. And just so we're clear, Doc, I don't trust you at all."

At the top of the steps, Grace turned around. Cole was still standing at the bottom, all tall and wicked and undeniably breath-stealing. Had she made a huge mistake in asking him here? Trying to work with him instead of against him? Clearly, she had an innate weakness for bad boys. One she'd thought she'd left behind in the dorms half a decade ago. But obviously that attraction to unreliable charm was back—with menace and fortitude.

And tats.

She inhaled deeply. *Come on, Grace. Shake it off. Get a clue.* This was important, what she was trying to do for her father. And she wasn't going to allow some silly attraction to ruin the chance to keep her father's last years comfortable and stable and healthy.

"I'll see you inside, Cole," she said, then turned on her heel and headed for the house, the tomcat's mating call behind her on the breeze.

Three

Not surprisingly, the vet had one of those homes that reeked of cute and quaint and nesting. Yellow cottage with red shutters on a nice bit of land, a couple of bedrooms, probably painted pale blue with lots of white bed stuff. Not that he'd seen the bedrooms. Or was planning on it. He was just guessing by how the living room and kitchen looked. Brick fireplace as the focus, not a TV. Seriously, how did she watch the Cowboys? Couches and chair, worn leather and prints. Clean and comfortably neat. And it smelled good. Well, everything except the long-eared thing that had attacked him the minute he'd stepped inside the house.

Now that thing's head was resting on his thigh. *Damn dog*, Cole thought as he stroked her head and massive ears.

The vet entered the room from the kitchen. After telling him to take a seat, she'd hustled her fine ass in there and started brewing up something. Coffee or tea, looked like from the two steaming mugs in her hand. *Yeah, buddy, focus on her hands. Nothing else is safe.* Her face held too many emotions. Same with the gorgeous green eyes framed by the longest damn lashes in the world. Then there was everything from the neck down. Jeans that took every sexy curve at ninety miles an hour. Bare feet. Shit. Nothing sexier than bare feet. Except maybe fitted tank tops with a hint of pale pink bra showing.

"Coffee?" she asked, rounding the table before the couch.

He shook his head. He loved coffee, and that shit smelled really good. But he wasn't getting any more comfortable here than was necessary. Miss Secrets and Restraining Order was trouble. He wanted to hear what she had to say, then get out.

"You gonna tell me why I'm here, or should I guess?" he said in a terse tone.

She placed the coffee before him on the table, then slipped into the chair to his right, curled her leg underneath her. "Do you have somewhere to be, Mr. Cavanaugh?"

His eyes narrowed. Why wasn't his asshole attitude putting her off today? Seriously, what was she playing at?

"Belle looks very content," she added, sipping her coffee.

"She's droolin' on my pants."

"And that bothers you?"

" 'Course it bothers me."

"And to think," she said evenly, "you were so interested in adopting her. What could have changed, I wonder?"

"Didn't know how much she drooled?" Yeah, the adopting thing. It had been his cover, his lie, to get into her office and find out where her father was being stashed. Who would've thought the long-eared drooler would get under his skin, make him wonder if he could handle being a dog owner.

"I suppose I could order her to get down," Grace remarked, then grimaced. "It's just, she's been through so much—"

Nostrils flared, Cole ground out, "Right. Okay, Doc. We both know the dog's fine. But my patience with you is wearing real thin."

Her eyes lost their momentary luster and she released a weighty sigh. "I've decided to help you."

"Help me with what?"

She didn't get to the point right away. Which seemed to be her way of not dealing with the hard or uncomfortable shit. "You need to understand, I was just trying to protect my dad."

"Not following you, honey. And now Belle here is snoring—so you'd better speak up."

"I still want to protect my dad—" She pushed

on as though he hadn't said a thing. "His good name. But I also want to help you. You and your brothers, and Mac. I want to help you find out what happened to your sister."

Cole flinched, and every muscle in his body tensed. This wasn't what he'd expected. An offer to "help." She'd tried to keep him away from her father, and from the truth—had put out a restraining order, for fuck's sake. Why the complete turnaround? What was she doing?

"How're you going to help us?" he asked. "What do you have to offer now that your dad isn't really . . . all there upstairs?"

It was her turn to flinch. "I'm not exactly sure. We can visit him again. Try again. Maybe Mr. Palmer—"

"Palmer isn't having visitors," he finished. "Won't talk to anyone. Deac tried. Can't get any info off the bastard."

She looked a little stunned by this. "Well, then Mrs. Palmer and their daughter—"

"Are not working at the bakery." He sniffed at her. "Albert Lee's had to close the place until he can find someone else. Christ Almighty. You know less about this town than me, and I've been in Austin training for the past two days."

She bit her lip and looked like she was struggling internally. But after a moment, the hard lines around her mouth smoothed and she blinked at him. "We could find the boy."

A hum started deep in Cole's gut. "What boy?" he ground out. Though he knew. He knew exactly who she meant. And when she'd said the word, his head had nearly exploded.

"The one who came to River Black," she continued. "The boy your sister liked."

With gentle hands, he eased Belle off his lap. "How do you know about that? About him?"

Her gaze fell and she stared into her coffee cup. "You asked my dad about him the day you . . . visited," she nearly whispered.

"The sheriff remembered that, did he?"

"He has his moments." Her eyes came up. They were wide and worried and confused.

"And in those moments did he give you any clue who the boy was? Is?"

"If he had, I'd have already gone looking. I would've told you and your brothers."

He grinned darkly. "Really?"

"Yes, really." She hesitated then. "You don't know who he is, right? What happened to him?"

"Happened to him?" Cole repeated with a snort. "Shit, Doc. No one even knew his real name. Cass called him Sweet."

"But you tried to look for him . . ."

He gave her a sharp glare. Years and years of looking, digging, asking, praying. Nothing. His mouth thinned. "What are you doing, Doc? And why?"

She bit her lip. "What do you mean?"

"There was nothing you wanted less than to help me."

"That's not true. What I wanted—what I still want—is to keep my father safe and protected." Her eyes tried to pierce the brick wall he'd erected. "But you believe he's a part of Cass's disappearance. That he knows something."

"Oh yeah," he said without hesitation.

She blanched, but pressed on. "So I propose working together, instead of against each other. Sharing information. You want to find out the truth about your sister's murder, and I want to prove my father had nothing to do with it."

Cole felt as if he'd been sucker-punched. It was the words "sister's murder" that did it. Always did it. This woman . . . this woman who had fought with him, avoided him, treated him like a criminal— which maybe he was sorta guilty of—now wanted to partner up. He couldn't imagine it. What? The Dynamic Duo of Death and Destruction?

"What do you think?" she asked.

"I think it's batshit crazy."

"So you'll do it, then."

He looked at her funny. Couldn't tell if she was serious or playing around. Hard to know with this woman.

She shrugged. "Batshit crazy seems to be how you roll, Cobra."

His chest tightened and one pale brow lifted.

She knew what he was called in the ring. "You doing research on me, Doc?"

"A little," she admitted.

He sniffed, looked away. This was nuts. If he believed what she was selling, that she wanted to protect her father, prove his innocence, then why would she want to work with someone who believed the opposite? Then again . . .

He found her gaze again. Studied her. He'd have access to her father and to everything the ex-sheriff had on Palmer. Hell, if he didn't want to reveal something he found, then he wouldn't. He'd grown damn skilled at masking his thoughts and feelings.

He took a deep breath, blew it out. Then nodded. "Agreed."

"Oh." Relief seemed to wash over her. "Great. Okay." She started to get up. "Well, then . . . maybe tomorrow or the following day we could meet—"

"Tomorrow?" he interrupted with a dark laugh, staying exactly where he was.

"Well, yeah. We should start as soon as possible."

"Exactly. We start tonight."

Her eyes widened. "Tonight. But it's getting—"

"Needs to be tonight, darlin'. I have to get back to Austin tomorrow. Training. Not sure when I'm coming back. Day, days . . . week. After the fight."

"Your fight's next week, isn't it?"

He nodded. Wondered how much research she'd done on him. Maybe he'd do a little on her too. "You have a computer here?"

"Two laptops."

"Okay." He took a breath. "Let's start from the beginning. Granted, we've done it before, but let's go over newspapers, school records, anything we can find from that year. Good portion should be online. See who was new in town, new at school, all that."

"I have all of my father's files."

He glanced up, his gut starting to churn. "That so?"

She stared right back at him. "There's a ton of them."

"I'm sure."

"Never thought to look through them . . . until now."

"How lucky for me," he said, tone dangerous. "And hopefully for Cass."

She went pale. "They're in the garage."

He stood. "Well, let's start there."

She turned and headed for the door. When they were just passing through, she asked, "Did you eat? Dinner?"

"I ordered," he muttered to himself.

But she heard it. She turned and gave him a curious look, her green eyes touched with momentary humor. He didn't like it. Tension and anger, and maybe even a thread of unease, were much easier to deal with around her. "I was at the Bull's Eye with my family," he explained. "Ordered a burger. Didn't get the chance to eat it."

"Should I ask why?"

"Nope," he said, following her down the hallway.

"Okay . . ." She laughed softly. "Well, I don't have any meat in the house at the moment. In fact, the cupboards are pretty bare."

"Don't worry about it." Last thing he needed was her fixing him food. Or maybe the last thing he needed was her giving a shit if he ate at all. He didn't like it. Ex-Sheriff Hunter's daughter all thoughtful, soft . . .

"I'll make grilled cheese!" she announced brightly once they came to the front door. "Wait." She turned around. "Do you like grilled cheese?"

Christ. Who didn't like grilled cheese? "It's fine, but there's really no need."

"Actually, there is," she said. "I'm starving too."

"Didn't say I was starving—"

She moved past him, away from the front door, and the garage, no doubt. "Two grilled cheeses and some tomato soup coming up." She motioned for him to follow. "If we're pulling an all-nighter, we'll need our strength . . ."

Her words trailed off as they headed into the kitchen, but the phrase *all-nighter*, and the way her perfect ass was swinging from side to side as she walked, was trying to chip away at Cole's prefight abstinence brick wall.

He turned away and cursed as Belle trotted along happily beside him.

He loved this land. Loved it like a father loves a child. Not that he'd know what that felt like. But he could imagine.

Spying the moonlit house spread out in the distance, Blue urged Barbarella into a canter. The spirited red roan tossed her head, but irritatingly obliged. She was still pissed at him for taking off, staying at the motel out on Route 12 and leaving her unexercised for weeks.

"Had to clear my mind, Rella," he'd told her during tack-up.

She'd snorted at him, then refused the bit. The human equivalent of being flipped off.

"And talk with Cowgirl," he'd added.

The horse wasn't having any of his excuses. And maybe she didn't like the idea that he had been spilling his guts to another female. To a woman he'd never met—and probably never would. A woman he hadn't been able to stop thinking about for months now. A woman who got him, made him feel understood. Someone he could trust in a time when he couldn't trust anyone.

Passing by the house, Blue noticed the light from the kitchen blazed warmly. He should be talking to *her*. His mom. Needed to have it out with her. Know the truth about her affair with Everett Cavanaugh. His gut tightened at the idea.

Was he ready to hear the truth? And after keeping it a secret, all these years, that Everett—his mentor, friend, and fellow cowboy—was his father, could she be counted on to give it to him?

"How long you been out there?" Frank called to him as he came to a halt at the barn door.

The young cowboy was barely out of high school, but he was one of the best hands Blue had ever seen. Whoever took this place on had better recognize that.

"Since 'bout noon," Blue answered, dismounting. "Was out fixing fences near the oaks."

The cowboy whistled through his teeth. "Damn. How'd you find your way back in the dark?"

Blue chuckled. "Could do it with my eyes closed. So could Barbarella here. We know every inch of this ranch like it's the back of my hand. Like it's . . ." *Mine. My home.*

When Blue didn't finish the thought aloud, Frank pressed, "Like what?"

"Nothing." He led Rella into the barn and into her stall. Sure, he was back at the Triple C, doing what he'd been doing since he and his mom came to live there. But it didn't mean anything was decided or settled. Not with his mom, not with his three newly discovered brothers, and not with the fate of the Triple C.

"None of the Cavanaughs are around, if you're looking for 'em," Frank called before heading into the barn's small office.

Blue knew exactly where they were. And he wasn't looking for them. They'd gone to the Bull's Eye with their women. No doubt they were having a few beers as they discussed his future. The ranch's future. Well, they could talk all they wanted. But the only one deciding Blue Cavanaugh's future would be himself.

Yeah, that's right. I said it.

Blue. Cavanaugh.

Four

They'd set up camp in Grace's well-lit and very organized garage. A medium-sized card table held their grilled cheeses and steaming soup. Cole was sitting on one of the chairs tucked into the table, laptop resting on his denim-clad thighs. Not surprisingly, Belle was fixed to his side. As Grace watched from her perch atop three massive boxes belonging to her father, Cole broke off a piece of his grilled cheese and fed it to the smitten basset.

"You're going to spoil her," she called down.

Cole's focus remained on the screen before him. "Don't know what you're talking about, Doc."

A smile touched her lips—quite without her permission—and she reminded him of their conversation a few weeks earlier. "Remember, you don't have space for her."

"Shhh . . ." This time he looked up, his eyes heavy with concern. "She doesn't need to hear that."

"Listen, Champ—"

"You know I don't like you calling me that."

Grace continued without stopping for breath. "It's important she hear the truth. Not get her hopes up with all your charms and sweet gestures."

His brows drew up. "I have charms?"

Oh, he was such a pain. "You know how charming you can be, Cole Cavanaugh. And rejection can be very devastating to a girl."

Predatory black eyes surrounded by long, pale lashes seized her gaze. The look sent a strange shiver up her spine. She wondered if he stared at his opponents that way. Or the women in his life. Or both.

"I'm not rejecting her, Grace," he said coolly. "My life doesn't allow for her. That's a very different thing."

"Not really." *Not to a girl.*

"What do you mean?"

"Clearly you don't know the female species."

Those dark eyes flashed with wicked intent and a smile curved his mouth. "Oh, make no mistake, Doc. I know the female species."

Grace swallowed. Good Lord. Along with the shiver making its way up her spine, a blast of heat and unwanted awareness snaked through her belly. Charming—and dangerous. She'd have to watch that as they worked together. There was no way she was going to let herself fall for another player. Especially one who wanted to get to her father—not get into her pants.

Heat rushed up her neck and into her face. Thankfully, Cole was already back looking at his computer, or she was pretty damn sure he would be remarking on her lobster-colored cheeks.

She studied him for a moment. Brow furrowed, thick fingers stabbing away at the keyboard, intense gaze. Besides being a fine-looking man who wore ink as well as he wore denim and T-shirts rolled up at the sleeves, he fairly oozed masculinity and strength. Her eyes moved up, watching as the cords of muscles in his forearms strained and flexed. Completely unwanted, an image of him lifting her up and placing her over his shoulder before walking off somewhere private flashed into her mind.

"You going to stare at me, Doc?" he asked, his eyes trained on the screen. "Or get to work?"

Lobster cheeks were on fire now.

"I am not staring," she lied, clearing her throat and returning to the box in front of her. "I was wondering if you'd found something. You looked transfixed."

"No." His reply was more of a grumble.

"Okay, what's wrong, then?" she asked, searching through files for the months surrounding Cass's abduction. "And don't say you're still hungry. I'm not making another grilled cheese just so you can feed it to Belle. She's getting a little full around the middle as it is."

"I'm not hungry," he said tightly. "And Belle is fine. You shouldn't say shit like that around her. Don't want to give her any body image issues."

Grace looked up in surprise and interest.

He still stared at the screen, but his lip was curled. "Maybe you're the one who doesn't know females, Dr. Hunter."

Granted, she loved that he was championing the basset the way he was, but she had a sneaking suspicion his irritation stemmed from more than her comment regarding Belle's weight. "Care to share?" she asked.

"Share what?" he replied, gaze still fixed intently on the screen.

"What's got a bug up your ass? From the moment you walked in here, you've been angry with me." She released a breath. "Look, I'm sorry about the restraining order. But you should be sorry too. What you did was wrong. Now, I'm all for putting that behind us and working together without anger and frustration. Are you?"

He snapped the laptop closed. "I don't know what I am. But I do know I'm not finding anything. No articles about the case I haven't seen or read a hundred times." He growled softly. "Not sure why I thought there might be something. Everyone looked for this Sweet asshole, and they came up with nothing." He set the laptop on the table beside the not-so-steaming-anymore soup and looked up at her. "What are we doing?"

Behind his eyes she saw worry, and maybe just a hint of fear. Did he want to know the truth? Or, like her, was he scared to know it?

"We've only been at it an hour, Champ."

His jaw tightened. "I asked you not to call me that."

"Okay, I won't. But can I ask . . . is it bad luck or something?"

"No. Just don't like you saying it."

"Me or anyone?"

"You ask too many questions."

She shrugged. "I think that's another female thing."

He pushed away from the table and stood up. He looked twitchy, on edge. "I need some air. I need . . . to do something."

Grace watched him. She'd seen enough animals in her life to know when they felt caged.

"When I'm in training mode, I'm restless," he explained. "I need to use up excess energy constantly. Emotions are running high, that sort of thing. And with what we're doing here . . . what's been happening since my dad died . . ."

"I get it," she said quickly. And she did. She'd lost someone so close to her that at times it had felt like a limb was missing. What she couldn't imagine was how it would feel to not know what had happened to that person . . . "You want to take off? Pick this up later—?"

"No."

She watched him, watched as he paced the floor of the garage, the basset following along behind him. "Belle could use a walk," she suggested finally. "We haven't been out today. Her leash is right there on the peg by the door."

He stopped, caught her gaze, and stared at her hard, as if trying to read her, figure her out.

"What?" she asked.

He explored her face, cheeks, mouth . . . then came to rest once again on her eyes. He shook his head. "It's nothing. Just . . ." After a second, he seemed to think better of it. "Nothing. The grilled cheese was good. Soup too. I appreciate it."

"No problem." Confusion spilled through her as well. What was that look about? What had he been about to say?

He went to the door, grabbed the leash. Belle trotted after him eagerly and sat very still as he snapped her in. Grace imagined a good percentage of the female species reacted like that to Cole Cavanaugh.

Before walking out the door, he glanced back at Grace. "You gonna stay here?"

"Yeah. There may be nothing to find on the web, but we have a lot of boxes to go through."

His gaze shifted to the stack. "I'll be back in thirty."

"Take your time."

His eyes found hers once again, and in them she saw conflict stirring. No doubt he was wondering why she was being so accommodating, kind, forgiving. Why she didn't think he was weird for needing to rush outside and work off some pent-up energy. Or maybe he believed this—her, everything—was all a ploy to keep him close so that when information did come their way, she'd have a chance to vet it first.

He wouldn't be wrong on that last bit. But there was something about Cole Cavanaugh that tugged at her. Something that had nothing to do with his looks, brawn, or sharp attitude.

A shared past of loss, perhaps. A confused and shaky present?

"Clouds are full of water tonight," she said. "Go easy."

One side of his mouth quirked up. *As if I ever go easy, Doc,* he seemed to be saying. Then he gave her a nod, turned, and headed out into the night.

Cass was running beside him, moonlight bouncing off the trees, making her long blond hair glow. She was seven. They were seven, and Cole had blown off Deacon and James and given up his last summer night before school started to be with his twin. He'd never admit it to her—that would make him look all soft—but sometimes there was just nowhere he'd rather be than by her side. When they were together he felt whole, his missing puzzle piece set nicely in place.

Stars flickered in the sky overhead, and they joked and laughed their heads off as they followed the path of the stream. Their parents didn't like them out past eight, thought they'd get lost running around on Triple C land. But it just wasn't so. They knew every inch, every tree, every rock. Knew it like they knew each other.

"Watch it!" Cole called out, grabbing Cass and yanking her sideways just as she was about to face-plant into a massive rock.

She didn't even miss a step. "You're the best brother ever, Cole," she called out before turning around again and kicking up water with the tip of her boot. "But don't tell Deac and James I said so."

He'd granted her a deep grin. "I won't. Now watch where you're going."

"And my best friend," she kept on.

"But don't tell Mac, right?"

She laughed. "Right." Dancing her way up the small incline, she called back, "Hey, Cole?"

"Yup?"

"You think we'll be friends when we're all grown up?"

"Heck, no," he tossed out as a couple of squirrels gave chase up a tree to his right.

Cass stopped and stared at him, hands on her hips. Under the bright September moonlight, her black eyes glowed with mock fury. Or at least he thought it was mock. Sometimes it was hard to tell with Cass.

Cole laughed. "Come on. You know I'm kidding. We're family, girl."

For a second, she looked unconvinced, narrowed her eyes at him in a real show of vehemence. But after a moment she deflated, shook her head, and took off downstream at a bit of a gallop.

Cole followed her with a grin. He loved messing with his twin. Maybe it was because he was a gigantic jerk. Or maybe it was because he needed to be assured that she loved him, relied on him, needed him.

But when I did need you, you weren't there for me.

"Cass!" he shouted.

Lightning erupted in the sky, answering him, stealing his thoughts and memories—and torment. Chest tight, he stood stock-still in the center of the open field at the very edge of Grace's property. Clouds now blocked out the moon entirely, gunmetal and threatening. How long had he been out here? He glanced down at Belle. She was sitting on her butt staring up at him, eyes wide as if to say, *What's your problem, buddy?*

He swallowed thickly and inhaled. "Just losing my mind, is all."

She cocked her head to the side.

"Cass has always been with me. In high school, after I left River Black, in the ring. Outside the ring, watching me as I took out her murderer over and over again. But lately . . ." Since all this had gotten dredged up again, when she was with him, in his mind, she wasn't soft and playful. She was accusatory and frightened.

He turned around and headed in the direction of the house at a light jog. "I don't know if I want to hear the truth," he muttered aloud. "Shit, that's not exactly right. I want to know the truth, but . . . I'm fucking scared to know it. Scared of what I'm going to do to anyone who was involved." *Palmer, Sheriff Hunter . . .*

Entering the dark woods, Belle barked up at him, a low, funny howling sound that made him smile. Sadly. Bitterly. "You think I'm nuts too, don't you, girl?"

The basset never answered him. Or if she did, Cole didn't hear it. Midstride, his foot caught on something—a felled log, maybe—and he went flying forward like goddamned Superman. Without the superpowers. Arms outstretched, he braced for impact, but saw Belle dart out in front of him. At the last second he twisted to avoid hitting her and slammed against a large rock. Knowing his body the way he did, he knew the second he hit dirt that his face was cut and bleeding. But worse, his left ankle was royally fucked up.

Five

Grace wasn't normally a clock-watcher. Even at work, she found herself ignoring the time when she was engrossed in a patient. But in the past fifteen minutes, as she dug through box after box, she'd glanced up at the garage wall seven times. Granted, Cole Cavanaugh was a big boy—bigger than most, going by muscle mass—and he could take care of himself on her twelve acres. But he had said he'd be back in a half hour.

A rumble of thunder sounded.

And rain was coming. Crap. Belle hated storms. In the weeks since the basset had been living at her place, Grace had witnessed her slip under the bed and howl softly when there was even a hint of a storm in the sky. Maybe Belle was the problem. Maybe she had heard the thunder, stopped right where she was—or climbed into a hollow log or under a bush—and refused to move. Cole probably wouldn't know how to coax her out. But Grace did believe that if the dog was scared, the man who pretended he wasn't completely taken by her wouldn't leave her.

Cursing softly, Grace climbed down from the boxes. She shouldn't have let Belle go with him. Should've locked her in the house. Where should she look first? Woods? Field? She slipped on a jacket, grabbed a flashlight and an umbrella, and headed out. No rain was falling just yet but, boy, was the sky distressed. Ominous gray clouds were moving swiftly, heavy and ready to burst. There wasn't much time. She needed to find them.

Rounding the house, she hurried across the back field and into the woods, calling both of their names as she went. Her place was vast, lots of trees, green, privacy, a stream running through it. After returning home to River Black from a clinical residency in San Antonio a year before, she'd craved a life on verdant property. But right that moment, under the cover of darkest night, silent lightning strikes and rumbles of thunder overhead, she wished she'd gone with the condo near town.

Nearing the edge of the forest, which looked unpromisingly black, she stopped and cupped her hands around her mouth. "Cole?" she yelled. "Belle!" But the reply was only wind whipping through the trees and another boom of thunder.

Flashlight up and near her ear, she left the open field and headed into the forest. High grasses brushed her legs, and the soles of her boots made squishing sounds over the muddy ground. Inhaling deeply, she smelled the familiar scent of the stream. Most people tended to walk alongside water when it was available. Just human nature.

A familiar howl rushed her way on the wind as she neared the footbridge. Her heart jumped inside her chest and she cried, "Belle! Cole! Where are you guys?"

Another howl sounded. Then another. She followed it, tracked it. "Belle!"

The first sprinkles of the coming rain had hit the back of her neck when Cole's voice exploded through the forest.

"We're here!" he shouted. "North side of the stream! Massive oak."

Grace took off, keeping the flashlight aloft. What had happened? Why were they stuck on the other side of the stream? Another howl sounded, then a series of barks. Closer. She was nearly upon them. A circle of yellow light hit her in the face, then quickly jerked away, capturing a shocking scene. Leaning against a tree, that mighty oak, his face scratched up and bloody, was Cole. Belle was pacing back and forth in front of him.

Grace's heart slammed into her throat. "What happened?" she demanded, her breathing labored.

"Running in the dark," was Cole's answer. He sounded pissed off. Not afraid or in pain.

She shined the flashlight in his face. "How hurt are you?"

"Ankle's blown . . ."

"And you have some facial lacerations," she finished, her gaze running over his cheek and jaw.

"Was trying to get back, but I couldn't move very fast. And I was injuring it further . . ."

Grace tucked her head under his arm so he could lean on her. "Come on," she urged, taking some of his weight—or trying, anyway. "Before the sky really opens up."

He turned to look at her, his face scraped and bloody, those dark eyes eating her up, examining her, probing her, even in the near blackness. When he looked at her like that, Grace felt her breath hitch in her throat.

"You sure that restraining order's been retracted?" he asked.

She swallowed thickly. She'd never noticed the scar near his right ear or the fullness of his lower lip. Should she be noticing them now?

Lightning crackled in the sky, causing Belle to howl again.

"We should go," Grace muttered.

"You think you can take my weight?" he asked, one eyebrow lifting.

He grinned. He looked strange, frightening in the dim light, but somehow . . . sexy. Heat sizzled in her belly. She mentally rolled her eyes; then, as the rain started to fall in real, true sheets of icy water, she led her battered and bruised guest back toward home.

Normally, Bossy Dr. Hunter pissed Cole off, but not tonight.

After arriving at her house, she'd helped him inside and into the closest bedroom. Then she'd taken off his clothes. Stripped him! Not so he was buck naked or anything. But pretty damn close. Down to his slightly damp boxer briefs. And even then, she'd taken a second to decide if she was going to yank off those too before ordering him into bed.

As the rain fell in torrents outside the window behind him, Cole watched her inspect him thoroughly, her cool, gentle hands cleaning up his face, before moving on to his ankle. The palpating hurt like a motherfucker, but if she went any higher—say, above the knee, she was going to get a big surprise. Yeah, that's right. Cole Cavanaugh could be bleeding, have a couple of broken bones—maybe even be close to death—and his plumbing would not only work, but work at a hundred damn percent.

A hundred and ten around this girl, he thought, eyeing her soaked tank top, which clung to her breasts, rib cage, and flat stomach. *Hundred twenty-five.* A low growl rumbled in his throat.

Not good. Not good at all.

Remember why you're here, asshole. And it's sure not to play doctor.

She glanced up then, her eyes concerned. "Hurt?"

"Sure," he said noncommittally. *Not in the way you think, but sure . . .*

"I'm going to wrap it." She reached around to grab her medical bag from the floor.

"Don't you think a doctor should be doing this?" *Like an old guy with cold hands and a bored expression.*

Her eyes met his and she looked slightly insulted. "I am a doctor."

"You're a vet," he countered.

She lifted her chin. "And you act like an animal most of the time, so I'd say it's a match made in heaven." Her thumb grazed the inside of his ankle.

"Made in hell, more like," he ground out.

"You feeling the pain now?" she asked innocently.

"Yup. The pain of being forced to lie here surrounded by all this pink."

She glanced up and around the room for a second. "It's pale pink," she said, turning back to him and gently placing the compression wrap around his ankle. "The palest pink ever."

"Still pink."

Her brow furrowed. "You're sounding like a guy who's not all that confident in his manhood."

Cole just laughed, and again wished for an ancient male doctor. *Honey,* he wanted to say, *if you would just drag those soft, warm hands a little higher, you'd bear witness to my manhood.* Every curious, overeager inch.

Forget the pink walls—he needed to get out of here, get back home . . . Well, he didn't exactly have one of those, but to the Triple C anyway.

"All right," she said after a moment. "I think we're done here." Avoiding looking at his bare chest or boxers, she put an ice pack on his ankle, then dragged the sheet over him.

Cole couldn't stop himself from looking—from running his gaze over her. Her dark hair was wet and slicked back on her face. It was a sharp, smart, beautiful face. The face of the enemy. Well, not the enemy exactly, but someone he needed to keep his guard up around. Someone he couldn't trust. Someone who was coaching for a team he wanted to take out. He breathed in, his nostrils filling with a scent that should be illegal. At least to a horny fighter. What was that? Soap, rain, a little sweat . . . damn if it didn't make his gut go tight. And the Florence Nightingale caretaking thing she had going on? Well, that was the veritable cherry on top of his sundae.

She was staring at him. Maybe wondering what he was thinking about. Or if he was hurting. Or if it made him at all uncomfortable that he was tucked into her bed with nothing on but a pair of boxers.

"What?" he asked her.

"How many times have you been hit?" she

asked him, her eyes moving over him. They were an incredible shade of green. Changed with the light, and with her mood. He'd never seen anything like them before.

"Too many times." He grinned. " 'Course, some might say not enough."

She smiled too. "Like that man you're going to fight next week?"

"Him, among others."

"Well, that's barbaric," she said.

"No. That's just me, Doc. Cole the Barbarian."

She laughed. Goddamn, it was a pretty sound. "Is that what I should call you instead of Champ?"

"Shit, anything's better than Champ," he said on a grumble.

"Why?"

He shrugged, didn't meet her gaze. "It's what a father calls his boy when they're having a soft moment. It's not a name for what I do."

"Did your father call you that?"

Cole felt a pull on his insides. *Lie. Just lie. She doesn't need to know anything about you or your past, or your daddy.* But instead, he caved to the moment. "Sometimes he did."

She smiled and nodded. "My dad called me Peanut. And Duckling and Green Bean, and the Pellet Princess—"

"Wait," he interrupted. "Pellet Princess? For real?"

"Oh yeah. I would've preferred Pellet Queen. I was that good with my BB gun."

Surprise coursed through him and he sat up a little bit. "You used to shoot?"

"Big-time."

"Where?" Here he was, getting personal, talking history.

"When I was in River Black," she began, her eyes lighting up at the memory. "I'd go down to Cory Craft's lake cabin. There was this—"

"Perfectly straight fence where you could line up cans," he finished for her.

Her eyes widened. "You've been there?"

"Only a thousand times."

For a few seconds, she just stared at him. As if she saw a few inches deeper into his skin. Cole wasn't sure if it bothered him or if he wanted her to probe further.

"How many you take down in one go?" he asked.

"Ten out of twelve was my best," she answered. "You?"

"Same. Ten out of twelve."

Her lips twitched. "Wow. I can't believe I never saw you. I would've remembered seeing you. Cute boy with skills." Her smile died as she realized what she'd said. Heat rushed into her cheeks and she reached down into her medical bag and grabbed a tube of something.

His eyes narrowed on the cream she squeezed onto her index finger. "What's that you got there? Something for a cow's udder?"

"No," she said, deadpan. "For a horse's ass." Then she looked up and grinned.

Struck momentarily dumb, Cole just stared at her. Then he started to laugh. Really laugh. In a way he hadn't done in a long time. The sound and feeling and the action drained some of the anger he'd been holding on to from earlier in the night at the Bull's Eye. It was a good feeling. *Light* . . . Shit, he hadn't felt light for a long time.

Grace leaned in then and rubbed the cream into each of the scrapes on his cheek. Cole didn't even flinch. He was too busy looking at her. Damn, she was pretty. Her dark hair slicked back, showing off a face free of makeup—a face that didn't need any. Most of the women Cole hung around with were heavily painted. Not that there was anything wrong with that. Just maybe, as he looked at this woman, he realized he preferred the natural thing. Or was it the Grace Hunter thing?

"Can't believe you tripped over a log," she said, sitting back and cleaning her hands with one of those wet wipes mamas used on their babies. "Fancy Feet Cole Cavanaugh." She raised a brow at him. "Hey, that's an interesting fighter's name. You like?"

"No."

She laughed. "All right, we'll keep thinking."

"We really don't have to," he said tightly. "And the tripping and falling thing I blame on the long-eared one."

Her brows lifted. "Belle? You're blaming this on Belle? You sure you want to do that?"

"Listen, I could've made a nice easy fall after tripping on that log, but she got in my way."

"Awww," she cooed.

"What?"

"You didn't want to fall on her."

"I'm not liking the tone, Dr. Hunter."

"What tone?"

"Excessively sweet. Goes hand in hand with this"—he gestured to the walls—"room and these sheets."

She feigned indignation. "I could've put you on the couch."

He lifted a brow. "Is that pink too?"

She tossed him a smug smile. "It's getting late, and you, injured fighter, need your beauty rest—"

"Hey—"

"And maybe an attitude adjustment," she concluded.

"I don't have an attitude."

"You're cranky." She stood up.

"That's nothing new, Doc," he said, tearing back the sheets and starting to get up. "I was born cranky."

She was on him in an instant, over him, her hands on his chest, keeping him in place. "What do you think you're doing?" she demanded.

He stared up at her, taking in that worried frown and concerned gaze. Granted, if he had a mind, he could be up on his feet before she had time to take another breath. Or—if he didn't have a soul—have her back to the mattress, and him looming over her.

Instead, he chose to stick with words. Boring-ass words.

After all, he had a fight next week—no point in tempting himself.

And then there was the sobering reality that her father may have been involved in Cass's disappearance.

"You said it was gettin' late." The heat and friction of her hand made his heart kick in his chest. "I should be going."

She looked down at him like he was crazy. "I didn't mean . . . You can't walk, much less drive. You'll stay here tonight."

His body reacted instantly. Tightening up. *Bastard*. Groaning with all the images that suggestion brought on. "Look, I can call Deac or James to come and get me—"

She pushed off of him and stood up. Her expression was a strange combination of weary and appalled. "The two of them are pretty much on their honeymoons. It would be incredibly rude to 'wake them up' late at night to come all the way out here to get you, don't you think?"

She'd made little air quotes for the "wake them up" part, as if she was really saying the couples were no doubt up to something dirty. Which they probably were.

"Sure," he agreed. "That's just a bonus."

Her eyes widened. "You're evil."

He laughed. "I know you're not just figuring that out now, Doc."

"You're staying here," she said, end of story. "You shouldn't be moving. Not tonight, anyway. You need to keep that foot iced and elevated. I'm going to get you something for the pain."

"Nope. Don't need it."

"Something like Advil will bring down the swelling, Cole."

"No meds go into my body this close to a fight," he explained. "And I don't need any cold on it either. I can handle the pain. Shit, I could probably drive if I had to."

"Well, you don't have to. You're staying right here in my bed." She went red and backed up a few feet. "Err . . . *the* bed. This bed. I won't be in it, of course. I have a guest room." She turned away and shook her head.

Cole grinned at her embarrassed rambling and let his gaze drop from hers and skim down her body. She had a small frame that housed the most delectable curves. Damn if her clothes weren't still wet and clinging to her. She hadn't even noticed. And he was supposed to sleep with her in the next room?

"What?" she demanded. "What are you think-ing?"

Not a chance. He wasn't letting her in on those kinds of thoughts. Shit. *He* didn't even want to know he had 'em. She wasn't a woman he could ever get involved with. Sheriff Hunter's daughter.

His hands went behind his head. "Just never slept in a pink bed before."

She looked relieved and took a deep breath. "Well, then this is your lucky day."

Right. Real lucky.

"Well, good night, Cole," she said, then turned and headed for the door.

"Night." Cole stared after her. As hot going as she was comin'.

"You call me if you need anything, okay?"

His mouth kicked up at the corners. "Sure thing, Doc." *Not in a million goddamned years.*

She turned off the light, then left the door ajar like he was a little kid afraid of the dark. When in truth what he was afraid of had just left the room. Sure, he'd found her attractive during their battle of wills and restraining orders. He wasn't blind to her charms and assets or the brain in her head—which frankly was the hugest turn-on of all—but he'd understood on some cellular level that she wasn't to be looked at as . . . well, a possibility. Da-tin' material. But now, as he lay here in her pink bed, smelling her on the pillows, his foot aching but the muscle between his legs aching far worse, he knew he needed to get out of this house tomorrow and get things back to the way they were with Dr. Grace Hunter. Annoyed, pushy, maybe working together, but with a mutual distrust.

Because any more time here, in her presence, under those watchful, intelligent, caring green eyes? And he was going to be in danger of letting down his guard and letting the enemy in.

Diary of Cassandra Cavanaugh

May 7, 2002

Dear Diary,

My birthday is coming up soon. Eeek! I'd like to have a big party. Invite who I want to invite. But Mama's set on doing it her way again. I almost told her about Sweet last night. Not about us. And how I feel about him. She would kill me then lock me in my room until my next birthday. But about the new boy in town who doesn't go to school while he's here, and doesn't get to make friends.

But that would be STUPID. Maybe I'd get him here to my party and all, but Mama would think he'd be a friend for Deac and James. I don't know. Seems like a big can of worms I don't wanna open.

Is it dumb that I want to show him off? Don't answer that.

Cass

P.S. Haven't felt like any eyes are on me the last couple of days. But I keep watching and waitin'. Bye-bye for now.

Six

The question was, how many times could an adult read the Harry Potter series before it got weird? Or embarrassing?

Five? Ten?

Do you really care? Grace asked herself as she closed *Chamber of Secrets* and opened up *Prisoner of Azkaban*. *The judgment of your reading choices is your own, babe.* Besides, nights like these were made for dipping into one of the best fantasy worlds of all time. Heavy rain, insomnia, and well . . . a hurt, gorgeous, tatted-up, mostly jerky man asleep in your bed in the next room.

Your pink bed.

She grimaced. It wasn't that pink, for goodness' sake. The shade was so pale it was hardly a color.

She glanced at the clock. One fifteen a.m. She had work in the morning. Patients. She needed to sleep. She scooted down deeper under the covers.

Her guest room was very comfortable. She'd decorated it herself in shabby chic. White and gray with accents of powder blue. Cole would've probably been more at home in it than the *pink*. But she hadn't thought of that when she'd helped him inside out of the pouring rain. She'd just taken him into her room without thinking. It had been the closest to the front door.

Her cheeks warmed. A man in her bed. That man. Nearly naked. All that muscle over smooth, inked-up skin.

Go to sleep, Grace. Go to sleep and stop thinking about things you shouldn't be thinking about. Strike that. About a certain *man* she shouldn't be thinking about. A man who—if he knew what she knew about her father—would be doing everything in his power to land him in jail after forcing an interrogation on him. Forget that the ex-sheriff was nearly senile.

Closing her book and placing it on the side table, Grace switched off her light. The sound of the rain, its steady fall, had her breathing deep and easy and her eyes closing. She knew she must've fallen asleep, for when she woke up she felt groggy and unsure of where she was. The rain still pounded the roof and the windows of the room. The guest room, she realized.

But what was that? The other sound? Belle? Was the dog having a bad dream?

She sat up, blinked. The room was dark, but

the pale light of the hallway spilled in from under the door. Her heart seized. There it was again. Not Belle. Yanking back the covers, she jumped out of bed and raced from the room. Deep moans echoed throughout the hallway. It was Cole. And he sounded like he was in pain. *Shit*. Maybe she should've called a GP to come out. Maybe she'd been too cocky about what she knew. And he'd been too stubborn about taking a few anti-inflammatories.

She opened the door in a rush, nearly upsetting Belle in her slumber on the rug, and hurried to his bedside. The light from the hall illuminated his form well enough. His massive, shirtless form. Eyes closed, he was definitely asleep. Dreaming about something awful—or was he in pain? This powerful, tattooed badass of a cowboy was groaning, writhing, fisting the covers, his stubbled jaw tight.

Her own hands balled into fists at her sides, she vacillated. Should she wake him? He was either dreaming about something disturbing or in pain. If it was the former, he could be moving around so much it could hurt his ankle further.

She leaned in and with gentle hands gripped his powerful shoulders. They felt smooth and dangerously solid against her palms and fingers.

"Cole," she whispered. "Cole, wake up. You're—"

The rest of what she was going to say came out in a rush of air. In one moment, her hands were on his shoulders; the next she had her back to the mattress and a man's thigh between her legs. Breath nearly knocked out of her lungs, she stared up into the drowsy, confused face of Cole Cavanaugh. For several long seconds, they just stared at each other, breathing heavy.

"Grace?" he uttered hoarsely, as if trying to remember where he was.

She nodded furiously. "Yes."

"Oh, Christ." He released her instantly, rolling onto his side. "Are you okay? Did I hurt you?"

"No." No, he hadn't. Hurt wasn't at all what she was feeling in that moment. Or what she'd felt lying beneath him.

"You sure?" he asked, his anxious gaze running over her face, her white tank top and fuchsia pajama bottoms in the dim light. "What were you doing in my room?"

"Well, it's my room actually," she chided with a half smile.

"Your pink-ass room," he added with a strange grin of his own. "Seriously, Grace. What's going on?"

"You were . . . making noises," she explained stupidly.

"Noises?"

"Groans."

His brow lifted and another hint of a grin touched his mouth. "I was groaning in my sleep?"

"Well, yes—"

"And you came in here to see about my groans?"

His tone made her shiver. "No. Not like that. Well . . . I don't know."

"I'm just trying to put the pieces together here, Doc. Woman comes into the room of a sleepin' man—a sleepin' man who's groaning—"

"You were having a nightmare, okay? Or you were hurt. I didn't know. But I wanted to make sure you were all right. There was nothing sexual about it, if that's what you're implying."

His expression dimmed. "A nightmare?"

"Or pain." She studied him. "Which was it?"

He didn't answer her. Instead, he rolled to his back. Grace's eyes moved over him. Waves of hard, tanned muscle. What would it feel like under her fingers? Beneath her palms? Against her lips?

Shocked and disgusted by her thoughts, she started to sit up. "I'll go now," she said. "Let you get back to sleep."

"Wait." Cole reached for her, wrapped his hand around her wrist. "No." Then he blew out a breath. "I mean—go, of course. Ah, shit, I don't know what I mean."

Confused, Grace turned to face him, rested her head in her palm. She wanted to ask him about his dream. It was clear that his troubled sleep wasn't due to the pain in his ankle. But she felt like he didn't want to go there with her. Could it have been about his sister? About her abduction? That must've wrecked all the Cavanaugh brothers, but the girl's twin especially.

"Is it the pink?" she asked finally.

He turned his head, looked over at her. "What's that?"

"Did your close proximity to this dreaded unmasculine color bring on the nightmares?"

She waited. Waited to see if he would open up or kick her out or pretend he didn't understand her humor. She really wouldn't blame him on the latter.

"You're kinda nuts, you know that?" he said, turning onto his side to face her.

"I do know. It's part of my charm. I mean, I'm the only one who thinks so at this point. Except for maybe Rudy, but—"

"Who's Rudy?"

"One of my vet techs."

Cole stared at her, something different crossing his features. Something she'd never seen in his expression before, and she couldn't name it.

"He finds weird charming," she continued. "Probably because he's weird."

"So he finds you charming."

"No." She laughed softly. "I mean, maybe. I don't know. How did we get on this subject?"

"The subject of Rudy? Or guys who have a thing for you?"

Her lips parted. "I didn't say he had a thing for me."

"I know. I did."

The thought of arguing the point, assuring the man not six inches away from her on the bed—her bed—seemed inane. Rudy was an employee and maybe a friend, nothing more. Not that it mattered. How she and Cole had gotten on this subject was anybody's guess, but she wasn't keen on continuing it.

"Ready for me to go back to my bed?" she asked, her chest a little tight.

"This is your bed, Doc."

The husky way he said it made her clear her throat. "You know what I mean."

"Yeah, I do. And no, I'm not."

Her heart jumped into her throat. "Why?"

He shifted his head on the pillow. Apart from his nearly skull-shaved blond hair, he was all dark eyes, hard cheekbones, a night's growth of beard around lips so full and dangerous and kissable they should come with a WARNING! HIGH VOLTAGE! sign.

"Let's just say I'm scared to be alone," he said.

"Is that the truth?" she whispered back.

"No," he returned with a serious look. "But can we just say it?"

A shiver moved up Grace's spine. He wanted her to stay. In her bed with him. Sleep next to him. Cole Cavanaugh. Champion fighter, ruffian extraordinaire. Partner in truth and fear. Sometimes charming, all times sexy, a problem she really shouldn't take on. So . . . yes or no? Stay or go? Pink or blue?

"What's wrong, Doc?" he asked, his eyes probing in the dim light.

Outside, the rain had tapered off to continual sprinkles against the windowpanes. "You're going to laugh at me."

Instead of saying, *No, of course I won't* or *Don't be silly*, he offered a very tough-ass "So what if I do?"

"I don't want you to laugh at me," she said simply. "It'll make me feel uncomfortable, and weird."

His lips ticked up at the corners. "But we've already established you're weird. Or Rudy has, at any rate."

"Argh . . . forget it," she said, starting to sit up again.

Cole reached for her and eased her back down to face him. This time, his expression was serious. "I won't laugh."

They were close. Closer than a moment ago. Too close. She chewed her lip, wondering if she could make something up real quick. Maybe something about needing the whole bed for her rare sleeping disease . . . or . . . *Fine.* "I've never slept in the same bed with a guy before." There. There it was. She'd said it.

Cue the laughter.

But there wasn't any. Not even a smirk. Only mild surprise. "Really?"

She nodded.

He didn't say anything for a moment, just continued to look at her.

"You think it's weird, right?" she said. God, why did she care?

"No, Doc," he said softly. "I think it's nice."

Nice.

Neither one of them said anything more. Neither one of them moved. Grace let her gaze travel from his eyes to his lips, then close. That's how she fell asleep, her face just inches away from the last man in the world she'd ever have believed would be her first.

Sleeping companion, that is.

Warmth infused Cole, and he sank deeper beneath the covers. He wanted more—more of whatever that was. Her? Had she stayed with him all night? Was it her skin that radiated such heat?

As his mind slowly returned to reality, he opened his eyes. White ceiling, pale pink walls, sunlit black-and-white photographs of dogs, a snoring basset hound beside him on the bed. Hadn't Belle been on the floor, on the rug, before he'd dropped off? How the hell had she gotten up here with those short legs? Maybe someone had slipped out and slipped the dog in. His gut pulled slightly. *So she didn't stick around. Big deal.* She wasn't meant to. She wasn't his. Christ . . . at most, she might become a friend.

"Good morning," her voice called to him from the doorway.

Cole turned, let his still slightly muddled gaze skim over her. She was freshly showered, wearing her scrubs and carrying a tray. Must be headed into work. Her pretty face was free of makeup, except maybe something glossing her lips. And her hair was down, hanging loose and lovely at her shoulders.

Yep. Friend. They could manage that now, couldn't they? After sharing a bed, airspace, a mutual love of BB guns.

He pushed out of his mind the strange urge he had to yank back the covers, leap from the bed, and kiss her, and instead called, "Mornin', Doc."

Her smile was a little shy as she came over to the bed and placed the tray down on his lap.

"What's this here?" he asked, taking in the covered plate.

"Breakfast."

"You didn't need to do that." He couldn't recall the last time someone had brought him breakfast in bed. Maybe because it was such an intimate thing to do—and Cole Cavanaugh steered clear of all things intimate. They brought on a desire to swap war stories, find weaknesses, root out emotions that were dead and buried. Like his sister.

"It's no trouble," she said. "How are you feeling?"

She meant his ankle. He moved it, tried to circle the foot. Grit his teeth against the pain that remained. *Son of a bitch.* "I'm fine."

Her brows lifted and she cocked her head to the side. "I don't believe you. Your face says different."

"Don't go analyzing me, Doc."

"Can I take a look, though?"

The woman was as stubborn as a tick. With immodesty born of years of locker rooms and weigh-ins, he pulled back the covers, trying not to cover up Belle, who was snoring like a buzz saw. Granted, she'd helped him undress last night. Checked him out thoroughly—well, his hurting parts anyway—but what was going on now was an altogether different kind of checking out. In fact, Cole thought with a dry grin, what the good doctor was doing could be considered ogling.

"My ankle's down there, Doc," he said with a soft chuckle.

Cole had never seen cheeks flush so fast. And such a pretty pink. Hmm . . . maybe the color was growing on him.

Her head came up and her eyes met his. She looked positively mortified.

"See something you like?" he asked.

Her eyes widened and her chin lifted haughtily. "I think you must've bumped your head, Cole. It's far too inflated this morning."

He grinned and picked up a piece of toast. "Nothing wrong with lookin' or admirin', Grace. I'm doing it right now, in fact."

She looked down at her scrubs as if she'd forgotten what she was wearing. "I have to go to work this morning."

"Yeah, I got that."

"But I'll be back by eleven. We can continue what we started before the unfortunate accident. Brainstorm on how we could locate Sweet. Maybe we can bring the boxes in here—"

"I can't stay, Doc," he cut in mildly. "I have to get to Austin. I've got training at noon."

She looked confused. "At noon? You can't possibly get there—"

"Deac's flyin' me in on his chopper. He's got some business there today."

"But your ankle is still inflamed."

He shrugged. "It's nothing." He'd trained on worse. Broken ribs, broken toe. Shit, the latter hurt worse than anything.

Her hands went to her hips. "How important is this fight next week?"

Cole exhaled. The fight. The goddamned fight with Fred Omega Fontana—the one bastard he'd never beaten. There was something about this fight, coming right now, when things were unsettled at the ranch and questions were being raised about Cass's murder. Before Everett's passing, beating Fontana was like beating anyone. A need to win, a need to feel strong and capable and feared. But now . . . it was as if Fred Fontana represented that faceless piece of shit who'd stolen his girl, his twin, his other half all those years ago. And every time he beat Cole, it was like letting Cass down again and again.

But next week, he'd make Cass proud.

He'd find a whisper of peace within his guilty, pained soul.

His eyes caught and held Grace's. "Why do you want to know?"

"Just wondering," she said lightly. "Because training on that ankle could easily make it worse. Give your opponent the advantage. So if this fight is as important as I'm guessing it is, you're better off resting another day." She shrugged. "Then hitting it hard tomorrow."

He raised a brow. "Hitting it hard, Doc?"

She shrugged. "Isn't that fighter speak? Hit it hard? Pound it in? Oh, I don't know. I saw *Rocky* once . . ." Her voice trailed off as she laughed softly at herself.

"You just want to keep me here, don't you?" he asked.

"Well . . ." she stammered.

"In your bed, I mean."

Her cheeks flushed again. Yep, pink was growing on him. And there it went, into his mind . . . wondering what else on her was flushing pink.

"I have to go," she said, backing up away from

him, like he was a bomb about to detonate. And maybe he was. "Clearly Belle has decided to stay with you instead of coming to work with me," she added, glancing at the still snoring dog, one long ear draped over her eyes.

"Puttin' her on guard duty?" he asked.

"I don't think you need a guard," she said, her back coming to rest against the door. "I think you'll always do what you want. No matter the consequences."

Some of the heat building inside him cooled. What did she mean by that? And why did she think she knew him? She didn't know him. Not even close. And she never would.

"It's up to you, of course," she concluded. "But I hope to see you when I get home."

When she was gone, down the hall, and out the front door, Cole swung his legs over the side of the bed. Granted, the woman had been good to him, setting him up, feeding him, doctoring as well as an animal doc could. But she didn't understand how things went in his world. You worked with and through injury.

He ignored the heaviness in his ankle as his feet touched down on wood. But what he couldn't ignore, as he stood up and walked around the side of the bed, was the pounding of blood and the ache. Sure, he could train on it. But the vet was right. If he injured it further, he was giving the advantage to Fontana. Anyone else and he'd go through with it—but he couldn't risk losing this match.

"Shit," he cursed. His eyes lifted. Belle was awake, though her head still rested on the blanket, and she was staring at him. "Yeah, yeah, I know."

He'd been bedbound only once in his life. After a three-week run of back-to-back fights. It's how he'd done things long ago when he was fighting underground. How he'd made his money—how he'd secured his rep. Hell, he'd slept for two days after that, waking up with one of his eyes fused shut.

Risking himself had been part of the fun. Going out there, seeing what he was made of, on one leg, hand messed up, eye blackened. But this was different. This was not about fun. It was about her. Cass. Fighting for her. He had to crush Fontana, and to do that he had to be in top form.

He was going back to bed. Grace's bed. Her warm and very pink world. But first he needed to pee.

He gritted his teeth and stood up, then headed for the bathroom.

Seven

"Just admit it," Mac accused in between bites of scrambled eggs with extra jalapeños. "You've been avoiding me."

Blue drained his glass of tomato juice, then set it back on the table. Mornings at Mirabelle's had been few and far between for him and Mac lately. He'd missed it. Hell, he'd missed her.

"Just giving a married woman her space, is all," he said with a shrug.

"Is that right?" she chided disbelievingly.

He picked up his fork, stabbed at his potatoes. "Yup."

"At work too?"

"What do you mean?" he asked before stuffing the three crispy spheres into his mouth.

"Just seems to me, cowboy, that not only are you avoiding your friend off the ranch, when you're on the ranch, you're ignoring your foreman too?"

"I do my job, Mac." He noticed his voice changed with his words. Grew a hair irritated.

"'Course you do," she agreed, glancing around the diner. "That ain't what I'm getting at." The place was packed. People stacked at the counter. She leaned in, her expression concerned. "Come on, Blue. Talk to me."

He knew what she wanted. He was no dope. She'd been after him for a while—to talk, share his feelings. Damn, why were women always after that? Then, once they had it, didn't much like how vulnerable it made the guy seem. "All right." He placed his fork down and grabbed his napkin. He swiped at his mouth. "I'd like to bring on another fifty head of cattle. Longhorns."

Her brow furrowed. That was not what she expected or wanted to hear from him. She shook her head and shrugged. "Okay. Sure. Fine. Whatever. You don't need my say-so for that."

He sat back in the booth. "Don't I?"

Her expression went positively clueless. "'Course not. What the hell is going on with you? I know it ain't got to do with your job. Are you pissed at me or something?"

"No."

"I don't believe you." She crossed her arms over her chest. "And for the record, if anyone should be pissed, it's me."

"How you figure, Foreman?"

"Well, for one thing, you never told me where

you went when you up and left town, or what you did—or what you're thinking now that you're back. You cut me out of your life." She chewed her lip for a sec, then huffed out a breath. "I didn't write that will, Blue. I didn't have an affair or lie to you about who your daddy was—"

"Quit it, Mac," he ground out, glancing around. The whole damn town looked at him funny as it was. Everett Cavanaugh's bastard.

But she was on a roll, and once she started she couldn't be stopped.

"I didn't threaten your place at the Triple, or offer you money to sell your share in it."

His gut went vise tight and his nostrils flared with anger. "You can tell your husband I haven't decided anything yet."

"This isn't coming from Deacon," she returned hotly. She tossed her napkin over her unfinished food. "Shit, Blue. Why can't you see me here? See your friend? Best friend once upon a time. Have I ever done anything to hurt you or topple your trust?"

For the first time since he'd been back in town, Blue really studied the woman sitting before him. She may have been married, living elsewhere, but she was Mac. Still crazy foreman of the Triple C Mac. The girl he'd known and befriended and counted on for a long damn time. *Shit . . .* What was it, then, that had him pulling away? Had him feeling distrustful? Couldn't just be who she was married to.

"Listen, Mac," he began. He took a deep breath,

let it out. "Something changed in me the day of Everett's funeral. And it had nothing to do with my sparkly brand-new last name."

"What?" She pushed him gently. "Whatever it is, I want to help. Listen, be there for you, whatever . . ."

He smiled, but he knew it wasn't rising up to his eyes. The smile was because he felt Mac in that moment. How things used to be. "I don't think I rightly know what it is," he said. "Just feels like one day I was living a good life, my dream, simple and real, you know?"

She nodded.

"And the next, it was gone. Dead as my new daddy."

"Oh, Blue . . ."

"I have an edge to me now, Mac. That wasn't there before. When I look in folks' eyes, I don't see the good like I used to. I see secrets and lies." He inhaled again. He hadn't meant to come here and talk about this shit. "I love my work here, love the Triple—love you, girl." When she gave him a smile, he tried one of his own. Still didn't work all that well. "Just know I feel like I don't belong."

Blue expected her to come back at him with something like, *'Course you do. You always will. It's your home.* But she surprised him by sighing and saying, "It was all so damn simple until that day, wasn't it?" Before he could respond, she laughed. "Remember when we had a few too many beers that Fourth of July back in 2010?"

"Dozen cows got loose?"

"Yep." She grinned. "For some reason we thought it was a good idea to not only bring 'em in and fix the fence, but paint the thing as well."

He snorted. "And you painted the cows instead."

"I painted *one* cow," she clarified. "Clearly, you were just too sauced to remember that you painted the other eleven."

Blue could not stop the smile that spread across his features. It was genuine and it filled his chest with something that felt like sunshine. She was right. Those days had been simple. In the best way.

He was about to tell her so, let her know he'd try to remember that as the gray cloud that followed along behind him most days opened up and battered him with cold-ass rain. But Mac was looking past him now, giving someone at the counter a friendly wave. Blue glanced over his shoulder. Stevie, Mirabelle's number one server, was handing a petite dark-haired woman some coffee in a to-go cup. Town vet, he believed. She'd had her practice up and running for only about a year.

"Hey, Grace," Mac called out. "Come on over."

The young woman's face split into a pretty smile, and she headed their way. Blue watched her progression between tables appreciatively. He may've been in a state of emotional torment, but that didn't stop him from looking. Woman was all curves and there was nothing a cowboy liked more.

"Morning," she said, coming to stand beside their table.

"Morning," Blue returned.

"Headed to work?" Mac asked.

She nodded. She looked nervous or pensive. Biting her lower lip.

"Don't worry," Mac said. "Cole isn't here. Can't believe what he did."

"What did he do?" Blue asked.

"Broke into her desk at the clinic," Mac told him.

"Those Cavanaugh brothers," Blue muttered dryly.

Mac shot him a look and he shrugged as if to say, *Trouble is as trouble does, darlin'*.

"Actually, Cole was over at my house last night," the vet said, heat surging into her cheeks.

Blue didn't think Mac could ever be stunned into silence, but there it was. Eyes wide, lips pressed together. Didn't last long, though.

"So that's where he went when he left the Bull's Eye." Mac shook her head, looked grim. "I am so sorry if he bothered you or pushed you or pressured you. It's true we're all looking for answers about Cass, but going to your house late at night uninvited—"

"He didn't," she said. Stumbled, really. "I mean . . . I asked him to come."

Bombshell number two, Blue thought, glancing at Mac for her reaction. This time all she did was whisper the word, *"Oh."*

An awkward moment passed. The vet sipped her coffee and looked around for anyone who might be listening but pretending not to listen. Lot of that going on around River Black. Big ears. Bigger mouths.

"Truth is," she began, "I want to—"

But it was all she got out before Mac's phone started making all sorts of noise against the table-top. She stared at it, then promptly snatched it up. "So sorry," she said to both Blue and Grace. "It's Deacon. He's heading to Austin today. I just need to ask him one thing about the house."

Grace's expression dimmed and she glanced at her watch. "No problem. I need to get going anyway. I have a patient in ten minutes."

"Okay." Mac seemed torn. But finally she nodded. "It was good to see you."

"You too." The woman gave Blue a smile. "Nice to see you again."

He touched the brim of his hat. "Likewise."

When she was gone and Mac had finished up with her texting back and forth, Blue felt the urge to inquire, "What was that all about?"

Her hand curled around her coffee cup and she lowered her voice. "Last night, we were all having dinner at the Bull's Eye, and Cole gets a text. Next thing I know he jumps up and leaves. None of us had a clue where he was going or why. Turns out he went over to the vet's house. Invited, mind you." She gazed at the door. "Very interesting."

"Who's 'we'?" Blue asked.

"What?" she answered distractedly.

"Who was all having dinner at the Bull's Eye?"

She shifted her gaze back to him. "Oh. Me, Sheridan, and all three of the Cavanaugh broth . . ." Her voice trailed off. She looked guilty. What she had to be guilty of, he didn't know. But it pissed him off nonetheless.

"Don't worry your pretty little head, darlin'," he said easily, pulling out his wallet. "I don't need to hang out with them to know who I am."

"Blue—"

He cut her off. Not because he was mad, but because there was something rumbling around inside him that needed to get out. A yearning. Or a deep sadness. He didn't want to study it hard.

"We should be getting back to the Triple." He stood up, tossed some cash on the table. "Even though no one's decided what to do with the place, some of us still have to run it."

At lunchtime, when Grace pulled into her long driveway and neared the house, she wasn't sure what to expect. A truck she recognized? An empty space where a truck had been because the fool owner had decided to do something stupid and head out to Austin for a training session that could injure him further? But a very sleek silver Mercedes parked just behind the truck? Hell, nearly kissing its bumper? Well, that was a shock and a mystery all wrapped up into one.

Who was here? And why? Sure wasn't a car she recognized.

She parked behind the Mercedes and hurried inside. The front door wasn't locked, but she didn't have time to question it as laughter nearly assaulted her. Male and female laughter.

Grace hated that her mind instantly went where it went. Granted, she was making assumptions. Cole Cavanaugh was a gorgeous, sexy, tattooed cowboy/fighter hybrid who seemed like a gigantic rogue. Loved women. Chased women—or maybe they chased him. Which accounted for the extreme confidence.

Point: He'd made a goddamn booty call while she'd been at work.

And worse? He hadn't even been considerate enough to get her out before Grace came home.

Red-hot fury rushed through her blood. *Guys are so predictable,* she thought as she headed down the hall. From high school to old age and everything in between. All they did was think with their—

"Well, there she is," Cole said as she entered the room prepared to do battle. And kick some naked female flesh out of his bed. Strike that: *her* bed.

But that wasn't the case. Wasn't the case at all.

"My savior," Cole continued, his dark eyes glittering with that ever present mischief.

He was still lying in her bed, propped up with pillows, wearing only his boxers, every superdefined muscle on display. *Except for maybe one*, she thought, then felt instantly disgusted with herself.

The woman who stood beside the bed had turned and was staring at her with interest. She matched her car perfectly. Tall, toned, and tan, she wore workout gear that clung to her amazing body and her short blond hair was tied back in a cute small ponytail. Grace had always held a secret hatred for tall girls. They could usually eat whatever they wanted and it would go to their boobs instead of their butt. Their legs looked amazing in heels. And . . . well, probably because she wanted to be one.

"You must be Grace," the woman said, extending her hand.

As she shook it, Grace snorted inwardly. Manicured nails too. Who was this broad?

As if hearing her thoughts, the woman offered, "I'm Katherine Vanderfield."

"One of my personal docs, Doc," Cole informed Grace with a grin.

Grace narrowed her eyes on him. Was he enjoying this? Watching the two women interact? Watching Grace's discomfort, and her cluelessness as to why Katherine Vander-whatever was in her house?

"It's nice to meet you," Grace said. "Welcome to my house. And presumably to River Black as well."

The woman smiled. Her teeth were very white and straight. "You caught me. I'm not from around here. My practice is in Dallas."

"You came all the way from Dallas?" Grace asked, surprised at the three-and-a-half- or four-hour-drive, while simultaneously wishing she didn't have all sorts of animal-related stains on her scrubs.

"Of course," Katherine said, turning back to the bed. "Anything for Cole."

Cole.

It wasn't that she'd called him by his first name that annoyed Grace. And frankly, Grace knew she shouldn't be annoyed by anything related to him. But if she was going to be annoyed, it would be by the very intimate tone the lovely doctor had used.

"I'm not throwing the fight for you, Kathy," Cole chided with that oh-so-charming grin of his. "By the way, how much are you putting on Fontana?"

Kathy looked shocked and appalled. Her hands went to her teeny-tiny waist. "I would never bet against you, Cole, and you know that."

"Better not," he growled. He was flirting with her. His doctor.

"So you're a fan of the fights?" Grace asked. "UFC and all that?"

The woman's pale blue eyes were kind, almost

pitying as she shifted them onto Grace. "I'm a fan of Cole's. He's got quite a large following."

They were probably sleeping together. "Mostly women, I'm guessing," Grace replied.

Those eyes turned to steel instantly. "I'm afraid I don't know the ratio."

Cole laughed. "I'm just glad someone out there is bettin' on me. Not that I don't like a challenge, mind. But it's nice to have the support."

"I'm sure," Grace agreed, then turned to regard the doctor. "Dr. Vander—" What was it again? *Vander-whatever* might not be the most polite way to address a guest, she thought.

"Field," the woman supplied with forced patience. "Katherine Vanderfield."

"Of course," Grace said. "I'm going to start on some lunch. Will you be staying?"

No. Say no. Of course, she'd had to ask. Good manners dictated it. But there was nothing Grace wanted less in that moment than to play hostess to Cole Cavanaugh's doctor/lover.

Thankfully, Katherine Vanderfield had other commitments. "I appreciate the offer, but I should be getting back."

"Thanks again for coming out, Kathy," Cole said.

"Anytime," she returned, flashing him that brilliant smile once again. Then she turned to Grace. "He should stay off the leg until tomorrow. Keep taking the anti-inflammatories. Then I think he'll be ready to get out of your hair and return to training."

Grace nearly rolled her eyes. "Sounds logical and reasonable."

Cole chuckled. "Grace here told me the same thing."

"Ahhh," Katherine said as sagely as humanly possible. "You were lucky to have such an intuitive veterinarian on hand when this occurred."

The image of brilliant white teeth cracking under the pressure of a tightly balled fist entered Grace's brain. She smiled, and felt Cole's eyes on her.

"Are you training at the same place, Cole?" the woman asked as she packed up her medical bag.

"Yup."

"I'll come out and check on you . . . say, Monday?"

The slow grin was back. "You don't have to—"

"I want to," she cut in passionately. "If I'm putting my money on you, I expect results." She gave him a wink, then turned and addressed Grace. "It was lovely to meet you, Grace. And thank you for taking such good care of our Cole."

"Yeah, no problem," Grace replied through tightly clenched teeth. *Our Cole.*

Before walking out the door, the woman glanced around. "This is a . . . sweet room. Yours?"

"It is."

"Love the pink." The words were kind, but the delivery was anything but.

As Grace followed her out of the room, she felt Cole's humor-filled gaze on her back. She wasn't sure why the situation she'd just found herself in bothered her as much as it did. Instead of leaving, going off to train, Cole had called his doctor to come and check his ankle. It was exactly the right thing to do. So what was her problem? Couldn't be the hot doctor who was walking out her front door and heading to her hot car with her perfectly proportioned hips swaying. She was around beautiful women all the time, like Mac and Sheridan. And it absolutely wasn't the fact that Doctor Hottie and Cole were probably more than just doctor/patient. Because that would be none of her business. So what was it?

She closed the door, headed back down the hallway. When she looked inside her room and spied Cole sitting up on the bed reading the newspaper, Belle beside him, the muscles in her belly tightened. He looked ridiculously hot. Yards of tan skin pulled tight around thick muscle. And then there were the tattoos. Intricate lines and symbols moving up both arms like curious fingers. Good God, what was she doing? Thinking? Had this territorial, jealous chick arisen inside her because of Cole Cavanaugh? As in . . . she was interested in the man? As in, she wanted to demand to know if Dr. Vander-whatever had not only brought that spare pair of boxer shorts he was wearing, but helped him put them on?

Heat surged into her cheeks and she wanted to melt into the woodwork around the door frame. Of course Cole took that opportunity to glance up. His eyes assessed her, and whatever he saw there made his brow furrow.

"You all right?" he asked.

Of course she was. Right as rain. Never better. Not at all confused about what had just happened or the strange bout of jealousy she'd just experienced over a man she was not and could not be interested in.

He was a fighter.

Virtually a criminal—he'd broken into her desk at her office.

An overly charming, oversexed flirt who would destroy her father in an instant if it got him what he wanted.

Look but don't touch, Doc, she warned herself. *Better yet, don't look. It'll just make you nuts. Just get to the work. To why he's here.* The serious, important, life-altering work.

She forced a calm expression and a light smile and walked into the room. "I'm fine, Mr. Cavanaugh."

He didn't look at all convinced. Maybe she should've left off the Mr. Cavanaugh part. "You're not angry that I called my doctor, are you? With the match coming up, I needed to make sure—"

"No, no," she assured him. Doctor? Lover? She wasn't mad. Couldn't be mad. "Of course not."

He nodded. "All right."

"So . . . have you eaten?"

"Not yet."

"The good doctor didn't bring you anything?" She just couldn't help herself. It was like the words were just bleeding from her mouth and she didn't know how to cauterize.

"Just some hard-core pain meds," he said, still studying her expression. "I took the anti-inflammatories, but that's it. Don't want anything messin' up my focus. Even when I'm feet-up."

"Well, how about some chicken salad?" she offered. "I think I have chips too. Maybe some lemonade."

He brought one knee up near his chest. "Grace, you don't have to do anything. Shit, you've done enough. I should be calling my brothers to come pick me up. Make them take care of my broken ass."

It was strange and a little frightening how quickly the urge to say no landed on her dry tongue. Maybe she should support that suggestion. Maybe, given how she was reacting, she needed to push Cole Cavanaugh away. "Why didn't you go with her?"

His brow lifted. "Who? Kathy?"

She nodded. *Pathetic. Seriously, Hunter. PATHETIC.*

For a moment, his eyes probed hers. Then a slow smile crept over his face and he shrugged. "She doesn't have a pink room."

Warmth seeped into her like honey. "Or access to the answers you seek," she added.

Truly, she hadn't meant the words as a dig. Or maybe unconsciously she had. But as soon as they were out of her mouth, she saw a hardness cross Cole's black eyes, turning them into two impervious stones.

She didn't like this Cole. He made her feel uneasy. As if she was standing on a small boat out to sea without a life preserver.

"I'll get the sandwich," she said, cutting off their eye contact and turning away. "Then I'll bring the boxes in here and we can get back to work. Back to the real reason you're here."

Eight

"It's funny," Cole remarked, placing another file on top of the stack to his right. "We all thought Cass would be in college before she even looked at a guy."

Grace glanced up from her own pile. "Really?"

They were both on the bed. Cole in his same spot, Grace across from him, near the foot. Belle on the floor, chewing on a stuffed cheeseburger dog toy.

He shrugged. "You know, no brother wants to think that about his sister. Especially his little sister."

"*Little* sister?"

"By a couple of minutes."

Her lips twitched with humor. "So she never mentioned the name Sweet? Not necessarily related to a guy?"

"No. Or not that I remember."

"But to Mac?"

"Yeah. He was mentioned. But not in detail."

"How is it possible that this young girl could be having a relationship—or meeting up with this stranger—and no one knows about it?"

The knot that had been forming inside Cole's stomach ever since they started going through Sheriff Hunter's paperwork twisted. "It isn't. That's why everyone thought she'd just made him up."

Grace was quiet for a moment sifting through papers, and Cole went back to his work. When he heard her laugh softly, he glanced up.

"What is it?" he asked.

"One of my essays from junior high. It's all about my love for Tex-Mex. Queso dip, specifically. It's a miracle I graduated, I swear."

"You didn't go local, right?" he asked. "I don't remember you. And I'm sure I would've remembered you."

Her cheeks flushed, but she shook her head at him. "You're such a flirt, Cole Cavanaugh."

"Wasn't flirtin', Doc. Least not that I'm aware of." His eyes moved over her. "Just telling the truth. If you went to school with me, I would've had a crush of my own to deal with."

She stared at the papers before her. "I went to a boarding school a few hours away from here."

"Why is that? Your family didn't think the River Black schools were good enough?"

"Wasn't my family. It was my dad." A sad look

crept over her face. "I went to River Black Elementary, but after my mom died I started acting out. Getting in fights at school—yep, badass Grace Hunter—stealing stuff from the store and from my friends. I wouldn't speak to my dad for days at a time." She shrugged. "I think he felt like I was falling apart. That maybe I needed time away from this town for a while."

If there was one thing Cole understood, it was loss. "Sorry about your mom," he said.

"Thanks."

"It sucks, doesn't it?"

Her eyes lifted again and connected with his. "Losing someone you love? Oh yeah. But I had my dad, and he was amazing." She laughed softly. "You know, when I finally let him be amazing. He worked so hard to keep me happy and engaged. After the debacle of junior high, he pushed me. Wouldn't let me turn my back on my goals even when things got hard."

Cole didn't say anything. What could he say? He wasn't going to be an asshole right now. Not when she was reliving her grief.

Her eyes implored him then. "I know you don't think so, but he's a good man, Cole."

"I'm not going to argue you that, Doc," he said, dropping back against the pillows. "I only come to this from what I know. What you've told me. What he's told me."

She paled. "He wouldn't have hurt your sister.

He isn't built like that. It's not in his DNA. I know it. And I will prove it."

Again he didn't answer.

"What?" she demanded, an ache in her voice he'd never heard before.

"Just don't want you feelin' disappointed, let down, is all. My daddy was no saint, but I didn't think he was capable of steppin' out on my mom, making a baby . . ." His jaw went tight. "Lying his ass off about it—and letting us all find out at his funeral."

She dropped her gaze, pretending to look through the contents of a faded red folder, but Cole had seen tears prick her eyes. She wasn't being honest, with herself or with him. She was worried—real worried. Maybe even suspected him, her pops. No doubt that was why she'd agreed to working together. Being close to Cole, seeing what he knew, intercepting information.

They all had shit they didn't want to face. But it was coming for them anyway. Best be prepared, and harden the heart. It had worked for him, he mused as he picked up another file. This one was thinner than the others, and the only thing inside was a faded newspaper. Cole eased it out and started thumbing through the yellowed pages. Community stuff, school sports . . . He was about to close it up and put it back when he spotted something on the lifestyle page. His family. His heart kicked inside his chest. There they were. At the River Black Fair. Mom was eating an ice-cream cone; Dad had his hand on her shoulder. All four kids were around them, eating ice cream too. Cole stared, entranced. He remembered that day. It had been a good day.

His eyes dropped to another picture below it. This one was of Barry Pickens and one of the Lansing kids, both atop horses in town. And to the right, sitting on the steps of the library, waving at the person taking the photograph, was Cass. Cole ran his fingers over the shot. Goddamn, he missed that girl. Would do anything to have her back. He'd failed her something awful.

Something caught his eye then and he drew the paper closer. What was that? Behind Cass on the steps, in the shadows? Or better yet, who was it? Didn't look like a guy . . . Cole turned back at the picture of his family, stared hard. His heart jumped in his ribs. What was going on here?

"What's wrong?"

Grace's concerned tone didn't pull him from the photographs. He brought the image even closer, wishing it was on the computer so he could enhance it. Fuzzy as it was, he could just make out a female shape . . . a skirt under the knees. He looked back and forth. He didn't recognize what he could see of the face.

He felt Grace beside him, camped out over his left shoulder. "You found something." It wasn't a question.

"A newspaper. Only thing in one of your daddy's folders."

She paled slightly.

"You recognize this person?" he asked, pointing.

Grace drew in close, studied it for a second. "No. Who is it?"

"Not a clue. But she's in the background of both pictures. Why would that be?"

"Were they taken on the same day?"

"No. We were at the fair in this one. And this one's out in front of the library steps. Besides, she's wearing different clothes. Hair's different too."

"It's a small town, Cole," she said. "Odds are you're going to be running into the same people . . ."

He knew that. He knew what he was seeing might be nothing at all. But it wasn't just what he was seeing. It was what he was feeling too. Wasn't right. Wasn't the guy they were looking for, true. But it wasn't right.

His eyes found hers. "Why do you think your daddy had this, Grace? And all by its lonesome in the file?"

She looked uncomfortable. Her face tense. "I don't know."

Christ. "We're gonna need to ask him."

She nodded. "Yeah."

He didn't say anything for a moment. What could he say? Your pops was in on this? Kept something hidden? Shit . . . she already knew that. It's why she'd suggested they work together.

He placed the newspaper flat on his thighs and

reached for his iPhone. He snapped a couple of pictures at different angles and ranges, then started texting.

"Who are you sending those to?" she asked, her voice sounding thin, worried.

"My brothers and Mac," he told her. "We'll see if any of them recognize her."

"But we're not looking for a girl, Cole," she said. "We're looking for a guy. The Sweet character."

"I know. And we'll continue to do that. But who's to say what will ultimately get us there? Cass's things, your daddy's things, whoever this is in the photograph. Everything's got to be on the table. Everything's got to be examined."

*   *   *

I wish I was there with you.

You could be. Can be.

Rules are rules.

I thought rules were made to be broken, Cowgirl.

Don't you like what we have? You can tell me anything.

Blue hesitated, his fingers over the keys. He did appreciate the mystery of his online relationship with Cowgirl. Since they'd "met" on a chat site for new, heat-tolerant breeds of cattle about a year earlier, it had been fun, exciting, comforting even. But things had changed so drastically in his life as of late. Now he wasn't content with texting or the mystery. He wanted to know her. No, he *needed* to know her—see her, touch her, talk to the one person on earth he felt he could trust.

Have I ever seen you? Have you ever seen me?

He waited on that one. Ten seconds. Thirty seconds. But there was no reply. Shit, what was he doing? Pushing her? They'd agreed to this relationship as is, and he was royally screwing it up. His gut contracted. He didn't want to lose her. His fingers hovered over the keys. He needed to undo this before it was too late. But then her one-word answer came.

Yes.

Nine

In the year Grace Hunter had been living in her house in River Black, she'd had maybe a handful of guests. She liked to keep her home private— just hers—tending to meet friends or dates in town. But in the past two days she was well on her way to doubling that handful.

"We're real sorry about this, Dr. Hunter."

Grace stood near the fireplace, the easy flames warming her thighs, and took in the two exceptionally handsome Cavanaugh men seated on her couch. "Grace—please," she told them.

Dressed in jeans and a faded blue T-shirt, James Cavanaugh stared up at her with eyes the color of the ocean and asked, "How long's he been here?"

"Since last night," Deacon answered him, then set his intimidating gaze on Grace. "Mac told me. I hope you don't mind."

"Of course not," she said.

The eldest Cavanaugh brother looked as if he'd just come from the boardroom inside his fancy office building in Dallas. Suit and tie alongside black boots and black Stetson. "We've come to take him off your hands," he said.

"You don't need to do that," Grace insisted.

"He's got to be a huge burden," James put in, setting his booted foot on his knee. "A huge pain in the ass—"

"I'm right here," Cole ground out.

Grace turned to look at the man seated in her leather chair, hurt ankle propped up on the coffee table. He'd put on a pair of sweats that his brothers had brought for him, but he'd refused a shirt. She was starting to wonder if that's how Cole Cavanaugh lived his life—shirtless. Hey, maybe that was the huge burden James had spoken of. Sans shirt, and what seemed like miles upon miles of tan, heavily muscled, intricately inked skin for her greedy eyes to peruse.

"If I'm not mistaken," James continued as if his brother hadn't said a word, "isn't he not legally allowed to be this close to you?"

Cole snorted.

"I took care of that," Grace said quickly. "It's been dropped."

James's brow went up. "Dropped."

"May I inquire why?" Deacon put in.

"No, you may not," Cole said brusquely. "It's none of your damn business. Either one of you."

"The hell it's not," James said, though his voice lacked heat. "This whole thing started because we're looking for the truth about what happened to Cass. Who happened to Cass. We're all in that search together."

"I agree," Grace stated evenly, her insides tensing up once again. Or maybe they hadn't stopped tensing after seeing the newspaper her father had kept all these years in Cole's hand. Lord, she prayed it was just a random thing, and not more evidence that he did in fact have something to do with Cass Cavanaugh's disappearance.

James turned to look at her then, his brows descending. "I didn't exactly mean you, Grace."

"Maybe not," she pressed on. "But I am a part of it now." They were all looking at her. Three sets of Cavanaugh eyes. It was daunting. She swallowed hard. "It's why I dropped the restraining order," she explained. "Granted, I don't love the way Cole tried to extract information from me, but I understand why he did it." She felt Cole's gaze narrow on her as he tried to figure out her motivation. "I want to work together. I want to find out the truth too."

"Why?" Deacon asked. It was a simple question, but heavy with significance.

"I want to know," she began, her heart once again ascending into her throat. "Make sure everyone knows—that my father had nothing to do with it."

She could feel Cole's eyes on her. Those dark, probing eyes. Would he tell his brothers about the newspaper?

"And you truly believe he didn't have something to do with it?" Deacon continued. There was no malice, no sarcasm in his tone. Just curiosity.

She nodded, though her chest was tight with tension and unease. "But he was around. And now his best friend claims to know something. I'm going to find out what that is."

"How?" James asked.

"We're looking through old newspapers now," Cole put in.

Grace held her breath.

"Right," Deacon said. "We got your text. Interesting, but I didn't recognize the girl."

Cole looked at James. "How 'bout you?"

James shook his head. "Why do you think that's significant anyway? The girl? I mean, we're looking for a guy."

"We're actually trying to find a lead on Sweet," Grace put in quickly.

"If he existed at all," James said under his breath.

"We gotta try what we can try," Cole said. "Palmer won't let us near him, so what does that leave us with?"

"My dad," Grace said, throat tightening. "I'm going to keep pressing him—"

Cole cut her off with one look. "I'm hoping you let me come along for that."

"Maybe we all could," Deacon added. "With more respect and honesty this time, of course."

"That's a possibility," Grace said, though her heart squeezed just thinking about it. What if he actually said something? Something incriminating. No . . . she couldn't allow that. She'd have to keep the Cavanaughs away. Occupied with something else. "Maybe I could get in and see Palmer," she suggested quickly. "He might be more receptive to me."

"After what he did to Sheridan," Cole said with a sneer, "I don't think you should be anywhere near that asshole."

"He's behind bars," Grace countered.

"I don't like it."

"It's not really up to you, is it?"

Tension rent the air, and for a full minute no one said anything. The fire crackled on, the wind picked up outside, and the night took hold. And Belle lay sprawled on her back on the rug near Cole's good foot.

Finally, Deacon broke the silence. "We appreciate all of this, Grace," he said. "And look forward to working together to end this long-standing, long-suffering mystery. Let our girl rest once and for all."

Grace's chest tightened again. She was telling them the truth. She would find out what happened— or try to anyway—but she would also protect her father, and his reputation and legacy in the process.

"Cole," Deacon started, "I'm going to Austin again tomorrow for a client meeting. I can give you a ride if you're up for it."

"Appreciate that," Cole returned. "I hope to be. Better be."

"In the meantime, why don't you come home with us? Take the burden off Dr. Hunter here."

"It ain't no burden," Cole said, sitting up now.

"Burdens don't know they're being burdens, little brother. That's why they're called burdens."

"Fuck you, Deac."

James's head came around fast and his voice was sharp as a blade. "Don't speak that way in front of a lady."

Tossing his hands in the air, Cole turned to Grace. "Do you see what I put up with, Doc? I'm five years old to them no matter how low my voice is, how tall I grow, or how much hair I have on my ball—"

"Cole, Christ Almighty!" James exploded. He eyed Grace, who was trying not to smile. "Say the word and we'll take him."

As Cole cursed and tossed his brothers a slew of threatening looks, Grace lost the battle. She couldn't help herself. Laughter bubbled in her throat. She didn't have siblings, and though she imagined at times it was a real pain in the neck, it also seemed like a gift. No matter how angry you got at each other, how you fought, they were still your blood. They were there for you. Had your back. Helped you when you were tired and scared and unsure if you were doing the right thing with an aging parent.

"Her silence speaks volumes," Deacon said with a hint of humor.

James nodded. "Should we toss him over our shoulder, then into the back of our truck, Dr. Hunter?"

"First, I'd say good luck with that—even with the hurt foot, he wrestles people for a living," she returned. "But truly, he's welcome here." It was surprising how easily the words rolled off her tongue. Probably because they were true. "It's really up to him."

Cole looked irritatingly chuffed. "That's right," he agreed with an arrogant twist to his mouth. "I'm welcome."

"Fine," Deacon said, tight-lipped. "Then I suppose the question becomes, why do you want to stay here, Cole?"

The arrogance in the blond man receded and was replaced by unease and impatience.

"Yeah," James said quickly. "Why do you want to stay at Grace's place, Champ?"

It was the strangest thing. That moment. Grace and Cole weren't even looking at each other. But completely unchecked, they both spoke at the exact same time.

"Don't call me that," he said.

"Don't call him that," she said.

The room fell silent again. Even the fire seemed only to smolder softly, mutedly. Grace turned to look at Cole. He was staring at her. Granted, maybe the other two Cavanaugh brothers were too, but she was hardly aware of their presence in that moment. Always deep, dark, and intense, Cole's eyes sought to understand her, take her in and read her thoughts. They asked, *Why? Why stick up for me? Why let me stay here? We barely know each other. We're playing for different teams. And there's that obvious attraction we're not dealing with.*

Grace had no answer for him. On any of those fronts. Hell, she was asking herself the very same things. Maybe she kind of liked him? Liked having him around? Maybe she liked their banter, liked watching him pretend he wasn't falling for the basset? Maybe it felt kind of good to have someone around who understood loss.

But then again, there were the downsides to having him limping around her house. Most of those centered around his appeal, his attractiveness. All that muscle, all those dark, intense stares. And the growing suspicion of what might be captive inside the mind of her father.

"I'm staying," Cole said, his eyes still pinned to hers. Then he inclined his head in the first show of Texas Gentleman she'd ever had from him. "That is, if you'll have me for another night, ma'am."

A thread of heat snaked through Grace's blood, warming her insides, and she gently pushed aside all the negatives of Cole Cavanaugh's presence. She heard one of his brothers mutter, *"Ma'am?"* under his breath in a confused tone as her mind rolled around the words "another night."

"Of course you can stay, Cole," she said in a voice that didn't sound like her own. It was breathy and warmer than necessary.

His mouth curved into a satisfied smile. "Thank you kindly, Doc."

"But I want you back in bed right now," she said without thinking. Then instantly wished she could take the words back. Or at the very least, burrow herself into the ground.

She'd meant to treat him like a patient—one who wanted to be up and ready to train tomorrow morning. But Cole wasn't looking at her like she was his doctor. His eyes had turned from deep, inky pools into two burning black suns that nearly stole her breath. Her eyes closed momentarily as she fought to keep all crazy and oh-so-wrong and inappropriate thoughts at bay.

"I think it's time to say good night." It was Cole's voice, rich and deep, and when Grace finally opened her eyes once again she realized he wasn't talking to her anymore. His narrowed and impatient gaze was fixed on his brothers. "Thanks for the clothes."

"Maybe you should put 'em on," James muttered, coming to his feet, righting his hat.

Deacon stood as well, but instead of talking to Cole, he gave Grace a serious look. "Call us if he gives you a problem."

Grace nearly smiled at that. Wasn't *Problem* Cole Cavanaugh's middle name? A guarantee if you chose to be around him. And clearly, she was choosing to be around him.

"I'm sorry you had to make the trip out here," she said, walking them to the door.

"It's nothing, Dr. Hunter. We wanted to check things out, and we did. And I'm glad we're going to be working together. Despite Cole's feelings on the matter, you should try to get in to see Palmer. It would be a huge coup for all of us. I think the effort will prove futile however, but stranger things have happened. When I get back from Austin, maybe we can meet with your father. Bring him a nice lunch. Make it relaxed and casual—no pressure." Nearly out the door and on the porch, Deacon turned to regard her. He lowered his voice so only she could hear him. "I feel it's my place to tell you that Cole's not really the kind of man a girl like you should be hanging around with."

Grace stared at him, almost too stunned to speak. But she managed to eke out a hoarse-sounding "He's your brother."

"I know. And I love him. Doesn't change what is."

"What kind of girl do you think I am, Mr. Cavanaugh?" she asked imperiously.

"A kind, smart, hometown girl who I got to believe recognizes bullshit when it's offered up." Without letting her reply, he tugged the brim of his Stetson, gave her a grim smile, then turned and followed James down the steps toward his truck.

Closing the door with a little too much force, Grace tried to decide how she felt about what she'd just heard. Annoyed? Insulted? The assessment of her. The warning about Cole. As if she didn't know what she had in her house. The overly confident tattooed arrogant pain in the ass. She fought the urge to grab the door handle and yank it back, holler after them. Tell them both that she didn't need their warning. That—*screw you*— she was a grown-up and could take care of herself. And that what went on in her heart, and potentially her bed, was her business.

Of course . . . that would mean she was admitting something could go on in her bed with Cole Cavanaugh. And she wasn't going to even contemplate that idea.

With a sigh, she turned to face the man in question—preparing herself to take in his hot, dark stare and waves of mouthwatering muscle once again. But the leather chair he'd just occupied not a moment before was empty, save for the indentation of his formidable ass. She glanced toward the kitchen and the hall. Had he gone back to her room? *His* room, she corrected. For now. Was that the bathroom sink running? For a moment she strained to hear, but then thought herself silly and started after him. They needed to talk. About the photograph. About the file. God, were there more files like that one?

A knock on the door halted her progress, and she groaned. *Damn brothers*, she thought as she turned and headed back. They really didn't trust Cole at all, did they? Or her ability to resist him? Unless they'd forgotten to give him his toiletry bag or something. She grinned at that. What would Cole Cavanaugh have in a toiletry bag? Toothbrush? Moisturizer? Bengay? Condoms?

"You'd better have a pizza with you," she called, yanking back the door. "Because that's the only way you're getting in—"

"Evenin', Grace."

"Wayne?" she said, surprised.

Standing on the other side of the threshold, dressed very handsomely in gray cords and a blue chambray shirt, was the always smiling, always cordial Reverend McCarron.

He took off his tan Stetson and gave her one of those smiles. "I didn't bring pizza. Was I supposed to?"

"I'm sorry, no. That wasn't for—" She glanced past him. The Cavanaughs weren't still out there, were they? Nope. No black truck in sight. She turned back to Wayne. "Never mind. What are you doing here?" She instantly wished for a rewind button. She was pretty sure that question had skirted the edges of shrill.

"We had a date tonight?"

Oh, shit.

When he saw her horrified, and no doubt embarrassed, expression, he attempted to hide his dismay. But he wasn't very good at hiding things. Emotions and desires especially. They seemed to flash like caution signs in his eyes whenever he spoke to her. His lips thinned. "You forgot."

"Of course not," Grace said emphatically. She forced a smile. "No. It's just . . . something . . . came up."

Instantly, the role of spiritual leader emerged within Wayne. He turned soft and pliable. "Oh, I hope it's nothing serious."

Before Grace could answer, a deep, masculine voice called out behind her, "Not serious at all, Reverend. Just a sprain. But thanks for the concern."

Cole knew it. Had known it from the first time he'd seen them together, sharing a booth at the Bull's Eye. The good and righteous Rev had a thing for the sexy, stubborn vet. Not that Cole could blame him. She was something to crush on, that was sure. Question was, did Grace have a thing for him too?

Something dark and alive rumbled in Cole's chest at the thought. Most likely the animal he let out of its cage only for fights. The thing was unpredictable and vicious, and for some reason Cole refused to acknowledge, it didn't like the idea of Grace Hunter taking up with the man who had just walked into her house like he'd been there before. Damn, Rev and Doc—that would be disappointing. Not because Cole wanted to take her out himself or anything—shit, that would be a disaster, her angel to his demon—but because Wayne McCarron was one dull son of a bitch. And no one should have to suffer through dull. Not for an evening. Not for a lifetime. Cole was probably going to hell for just thinking it. But then again, he was probably going to hell anyway.

Grace's green eyes were wary with a side of fierce as she watched him hobble over to the couch and plop his ass down, then set one of her daddy's boxes on the coffee table.

"You should be in bed," she scolded.

Oh, those words—that command—were working their way down his belly to places he couldn't acknowledge until after his fight with Fontana. And even then—with her—he wasn't going to be acknowledging them at all.

"Bed?" Wayne repeated, glancing from Grace to Cole, then back again.

Poor dull fool. She couldn't possibly be interested in pursuing someone like that.

Grace was trying to explain herself. "He's supposed to stay in my bed one more night and—"

"What?" Wayne exclaimed.

"Oh, no, no." Grace laughed nervously. "See, he

hurt his ankle last night and I let him stay here. In my . . . bed . . ."

"Good heavens," Wayne muttered, looking slightly sick to his stomach.

Cole shook his head, trying to suppress laughter. He almost felt sorry for the guy. "Listen, Your Holiness," he began sharply. "She's not sleeping there too, if that's what's worrying you. She's in the guest room. Left me with Casa Pink."

"That means 'pink house,' Cole," she told him, with a roll of her eyes. "Not 'pink room.'"

"Whatever. He gets the point. Don't you, Rev?"

For one second, the Rev's eyes skimmed Cole's naked chest and gray sweats, which were hanging a little low on his hips as he sprawled on the couch. He was just trying to be comfortable as he convalesced.

"Grace," Wayne said very slowly, turning his gaze back on the vet. "Seems like you were helping out someone in need. I think that's very good of you." The expression on his face changed. From shock and dismay to peaceful acceptance.

He'd decided Grace was doing the Lord's work, Cole mused. Or had convinced himself of that. Damn, the man was righteous. If Cole had showed up here ready for a date and some guy was sprawled out naked on the couch, he'd be inclined to use the old wrestling arm drag move and toss him right out on his ass.

"I'd still love to take you to dinner," Wayne

continued. "And if it's pizza you have a hankering for, it's pizza you'll get."

"How sweet," Cole muttered with a sneer.

Grace threw daggers at him with her eyes. "Yes, Wayne," she said. "I'd like that. But . . . I'm not . . . Can you give me a few minutes to get ready?"

"Of course," Wayne said graciously.

She's going? What? They had shit to do. Files . . . a game plan to get in to speak to her father about that newspaper he'd been saving.

"Please. Have a seat." She gestured to the couch and saw that Cole had taken it over. "Cole?"

"What?"

"Make some room. Or go back to your room."

His brow drifted up lazily. "Don't you mean *your* room?"

This time the look she threw him had a grenade attached.

"Fine. No sweat, Doc," he said, scooting over and pulling out a stack of papers from the box. "I'll even entertain your guest while you're gone making yourself pretty."

"She doesn't have to make herself into anything," Wayne said, his eyes warm and soft as he looked at Grace. "You're already beautiful."

Cole nearly puked.

Grace's smile was thin lipped. "Thank you."

"Sure, of course she is," Cole ground out. "But you know what I'm talking about, Rev. She's been at work most of the morning. Around animals. And you know what comes out of 'em?"

Wayne just stared at him, nonplussed.

Cole snorted. "Well, maybe she can explain it to you over dinner."

"Please ignore him, Wayne," Grace suggested.

"I'm sure that would be impossible," the man returned.

Cole grinned. *Not so pious after all. Little smart-ass in there . . .*

"Just do your best," she added, then turned and headed down the hall.

Cole gestured to the now unoccupied twelve inches of space on the couch. "Have a seat."

Wayne refused with a shake of the head, but said, "I'm sorry about your ankle, Mr. Cavanaugh. That must be a trying injury considering your line of work."

"It is," Cole agreed, grabbing another file and starting going through the contents. "And, Wayne?"

"Yes?"

"You know, we all went to school together."

One eyebrow lifted in question. "I'm sorry?"

Cole heaved a breath, closed the file, and grabbed another one. "Why are you calling me Mr. Cavanaugh? Like we're strangers?"

Wayne thought about this for a moment, then shrugged. "It's been a long time since you and your brothers have been back to River Black. It's almost like we're meeting again."

"Okeydoke," Cole said with a snort, his eyes running over the paperwork in the file in front of him. Meeting again. *Shoot.* He remembered pale-faced Wayne McCarron getting rejected by a girl in eighth grade and running off crying to the bathroom. Now, he wasn't going to say anything about that. But this man was taking his host and investigatory partner away tonight . . .

Cole's thoughts petered out as his gaze caught and held on a photograph at the very back of the file. It was the same photo he and Grace had found in the lifestyle section. Cass on the library steps with the girl in the background.

His heart started pumping, the pressure making his chest ache. Why the hell did Sheriff Hunter have this? What was he looking at? Looking for?

"Hey, Rev," he started, swiveling in his spot to make some real room for the man to sit. "Take a look at this, will ya? Do you know who this girl is?"

Instead of sitting, though, Wayne came around the back of the couch. He leaned over and pointed to the shot with his middle finger. "That one there? Behind the girl on the steps?"

"Yup."

He leaned in another few inches. "Looks like Natalie Palmer to me."

Cole's gut contracted. "Natalie—"

"Palmer?" came Grace's voice behind them.

Both men glanced up, forgetting for a moment what they'd just been discussing. Grace was standing there. All ready for a night on the town. *Damn*. The vet was undeniably a hot chick. Killer petite body, gorgeous face, expressive green eyes, long dark hair that made a man's fingers itch. But all of that was accentuated by the dress she'd put on. White and tight with little red flowers on it and a front that dipped into the most spectacular cleavage Cole had ever seen.

Wayne had noticed her too, and except for the rigid set of his jaw, was pretty much concealing his drool—as a righteous man of the cloth should, of course.

"What about the photograph?" Grace pressed, coming closer.

"Found it in one of your daddy's files," Cole said pointedly.

Her eyes shuttered. She was wondering just what the hell was going on too. And for a moment, Cole hoped the man wasn't involved in Cass's disappearance. For his daughter's sake.

Wayne cleared his throat. "It's hard to make out her face," he said, returning to the aged newspaper. "But see that mark running down her leg?"

Grace came over to the couch while Cole leaned in and narrowed his eyes. "What is that?" he asked.

"A scar," Wayne answered. "She's had it since she was five. Ran into a glass table and had to have over seventy stitches. She's become very self-conscious about it."

"How did you know that?" Cole demanded.

"She is a parishioner, Mr. Cavanaugh." It was all he said before standing up and addressing Grace. He kept his eyes on hers, didn't let them slip down to the paradise below her neck.

He was a true gentleman.

A man of God.

And Cole? Well, he was admittedly the devil incarnate—his gaze was taking in every sweet and creamy wave.

"Ready?" Wayne asked her politely.

"Yes." She glanced down at Cole. Concern warmed her eyes. "Will you be okay?"

He wanted to tell her that she shouldn't be taking off, with all they needed to do, with all they needed to talk about. And maybe he'd add in something about him being in a vulnerable, moderately pained state. But he didn't have the heart. She'd been good to him. Taken care of his pain-in-the-ass ass.

"I'll be fine," he said with a nod and a smile.

Something crossed her gaze, shadowed disappointment. But she recovered quickly. "I've left you a sandwich and some pasta salad in the fridge if you get hungry."

"How kind of you, Grace," Wayne put in.

Yeah, it was kind, Cole agreed. She was a good woman. A good woman who might've been born to a very bad man.

"I could call your brothers," she offered. "Get them to come back and keep you—"

"I'm going to keep working, darlin'. Keep diggin'," he said. His brow lifted. "Who knows what else I may find."

She paled at his words, but didn't say anything.

Cole glanced over at the reverend. "You take care of her, Father. Have her back at ten or you and me . . . we're going to have words."

Wayne blanched slightly, but still managed to try and set Cole straight. "I'm not a Father, Mr. Cavanaugh. That's a Catholic—"

"Don't worry about it, Wayne," Grace interrupted with a soft laugh. She slipped her arm through his and led him away from the couch. "He's just messing with you."

"What about the curfew?" Wayne asked. "He's not serious about that, is he?"

Again, she laughed as they headed for the door. "Come on." Then she glanced back at Cole. "Night."

His eyes searched hers for something that resembled a *Help me get out of this!* expression. But there was nothing. She was glad to be with Wayne. And why wouldn't she be? Sure, Cole considered the man dull as an unsharpened knife, but for someone who wanted a nice quiet life in River Black, he was probably the catch of the century. He clipped her a nod. "Night, Doc."

She gave him a smile. "Don't do anything that might put strain on your ankle, okay?"

She didn't wait for a response. Just turned around and was gone. Out the door and under the protection of the good Father Reverend. And Cole was alone with Belle and a helluva lot of files. He called the dog up onto the couch, then dug in to the box for another stack of potential clues, and most unwelcome memories.

...rt went from stuttering to the muscle

...up altogether. This was so dangerous.

...'t going there with him. Chit chat. Flirta-

...cussing her date with another guy like

...re two girlfriends over near empty glasses

...e. Cole Cavanaugh was just her injured

...guest/investigatory work partner.

..."n I get you something to drink?" she asked,

...to flee the scene. "A beer might go nice with

...izza?"

..."No, thanks," he said with just a hint of melan-

...ly. "Can't drink."

..."Oh, right. Training." She shrugged, then turned.

...Well, I'll get you a plate and a napkin, then."

...But before she could make her escape, Cole

...aught her hand and turned her back to face him.

Heart slamming inside her chest, she gazed down

at him. His expression was no longer relaxed,

playful. Instead, he wore a mask of dark curiosity.

"Something wrong?" she asked, trying not to

think about how amazing his hand felt against

hers. Strong, warm . . .

"He kiss you tonight? The Rev?"

God, this was a bad idea. She blew out a bre...

"What a question."

"Needs an answer."

"Does it?" She swallowed tig...

none of your business. I mean, ...

you kiss, now do I?" *Fancy Dallas*...

Ten

Grace found Cole and Belle outside in the back-yard when she returned home a few hours later. The former was seated at the antique glass-and-white-metal table she'd bought on eBay the year before, blond head bent over a stack of papers, broad shoulders and thickly muscled back exposed, and both feet on the ground. The tabletop was littered with about half a dozen candles, and when she approached and his head came up, those black eyes glittered in the firelight with quick interest.

Grace's heart skipped a beat or two inside her ribs and she moved his way. The man was terrifyingly sexy, overwhelmingly male. "How are you feeling?" she asked.

He sat back in his chair casually, his eyes moving over her. "Better."

"Really?"

One pale eyebrow drifted upward. "You sound disappointed."

"No. Of course I'm not disappointed." Unbidden, her gaze snaked down his neck to his inked chest, then shot quickly back upward. "Just surprised."

"I heal fast."

"You're lucky."

"Not saying I'm perfect, mind you—"

"No, please don't say that," she uttered dryly.

His lips twitched. "Point is, the ankle is now at eighty percent, and that means I'll be back to training tomorrow."

A lump the size of a grapefruit dropped into her gut. It was a strange reaction. One she wasn't sure she wanted to pick apart. "Well, that's great."

Cole was studying her. It always felt like he was studying her. For what, she wasn't sure. A clue to how she felt around him? Or what she was thinking? Why did he care? Unless what he wanted to ascertain had to do with her father. That made the most sense.

"Are we going to talk about those photographs?" he asked.

Her heart shrank inside her chest. Though she'd been thinking about it all night, she'd been hoping he hadn't. "I want to say that it's just a strange coincidence, but I can't. I can't say anything until I talk to him." She gave him a pointed look. "And I'm going to do that. Alone."

For a second Cole a[...] statement, but then he [...] His gaze dropped to the [...] whaddya got there?"

She looked down too. "O[...]

One brow lifted. "For me?[...]

She felt the muscles in her fa[...] tug at her lips. "Maybe."

"Awww . . . Rev was right abou[...] are sweet."

Heat surged into her cheeks. "It[...] Just in case you didn't eat your sandw[...]

"As a matter of fact," he said, eyes[...] hers. "I didn't eat my sandwich."

"Well, that's not very smart, Cole," she[...] in, forgetting all about her embarrassme[...] about the discussion she was going to ha[...] have with her father. "Making sure you h[...] enough calories is important to your—"

"You know, Doc," he interrupted, reaching up[...] and taking the pizza box from her hands. He placed it on the table beside him. "You're going to make someone a great wife."

Grace's heart stuttered at his words. "Excuse me?"

He shrugged casually. "You got the caretaking [g]ene, is all I'm sayin'. Not a lot of women have it. [Su]rprising but true." His gaze searched hers and [som]ething dark moved across the twin pools of [...] black. "I'm thinking the Rev might agree [...]e."

Her hea[...]
freezing [...]
She wasn[...]
tion. Di[...]
they we[...]
of win[...]
house[...]
"Ca[...]
ready[...]
the [...]
"[...]
cho[...]
"[...]

"Hey, I'll tell you. No one." He gave her a pointed look. "Training."

"Well, I'm sorry about that," she said idiotically. "For all of your . . . suffering."

For a second, he stared at her. Then he started to laugh. Really laugh. It was a rough-edged sound that snaked down her back, giving her a hot shiver.

"Come on now," he said finally. "Don't go running off. Sit with me. Watch me eat your leftover pizza."

"Watch you eat?"

"Yep."

Her lips twitched without her permission. "Sounds thrilling."

"Could be." His eyes glittered with cocky amusement. "I've heard I'm a sexy eater. Lots of tongue and teeth."

She tried to pretend like the breath wasn't stalled in her lungs. "That might be what's known as oversharing, Cole."

He just laughed again. "Come on, Doc. Sit."

"I should really—"

"What? Go inside and go to bed?"

"Maybe. It's been a long day." And at this rate, it was going to be a longer night. What was happening? Here? To them? A week ago she'd wanted to club him over the head. Now her mind was conjuring up all sorts of images that had nothing to do with retribution, and everything to do with her lips on his.

He pulled out the chair beside him. "Don't make me eat alone. Do that way too often as it is."

Nice touch. She was pretty sure he was laying it on thick. Making her feel sorry for him. She couldn't imagine he was ever alone. Not in the woman department, anyway. But even so she caved, sat down in the seat he offered and opened the pizza box.

It was a gorgeous night. So different from the one before. Clear skies. Bright moon. The scent of cool grass on the breeze, Belle's collar making that jangling sound as she sniffed herself into oblivion over by the pecan tree.

"This looks good," he remarked, grabbing a slice.

Her gaze shifted to the man beside her. Yes, he did. Too good. Cole Cavanaugh had this way about him . . . this thing that went far beyond his incredible looks and physique. Maybe it stemmed from confidence or a lack of caring what anyone thought of him. Or maybe it was his unwavering drive. Whatever it was, it unnerved her. Threw her world off its carefully constructed axis.

He glanced up then, a second before slipping the slice between his lips. "Pepperoni and black olive. This Rev or you?"

"Does it matter? It's untouched, I swear."

"Shit, woman. 'Course it matters."

"Why?"

He thought for a second, then shrugged. "I don't know."

She laughed. "How many times have you been hit in the head?"

"I think we've gone over this. More than you got toes on your feet."

Her mouth dropped open. She'd meant it as a joke. A comeback for his crazy questions about the pizza. "You've been hit in the head more than ten times?"

He shrugged. "Hit, kicked, dropped, slammed." He took a bite of the pizza and groaned. "Hot damn, I shouldn't be eating this shit . . . Christ, I sound like a woman."

She ignored the barb to her sex for the sake of keeping the conversation going. She never regretted pizza. Ever. "What's the problem?"

"Tastes like fucking heaven," he explained. "But it doesn't do a damn thing to build muscle. And don't get me started on all the salt."

She gestured at his chest. "You have plenty of muscle. I wouldn't worry."

A grin split his features. "Staring at my body, are you, Doc?" he teased.

She snorted, though her insides were humming with an uncomfortable awareness. "Kind of impossible not to. You're very anti-shirt."

"I run hot-blooded," he informed her before finishing off the slice of pizza.

She rolled her eyes.

"It's true. I think I'm part tiger."

"Or part dog," she returned.

Without warning, he leaned in and growled at her.

Shock waves of heat barreled through Grace. She stared at him. He was so close. Less than a foot away. Her breath was coming in shallow, and she wondered if slapping herself might bring back the calm, put-together Dr. Hunter. Or diving into a vat of ice water. She guessed not.

She cleared her throat. "Did you manage to do some more digging?" She hated that she'd asked him that, that she'd brought up the files, and the photograph again. But it was the only thing that might bring back their sanity.

He nodded. "Didn't find anything else, though. I e-mailed Mac about the picture. Asked her what she knew about Natalie during those years. We'll see if she has anything to add."

"Maybe they were friends?" she said, though it came out a whisper. "Natalie and Cass."

"I don't think so. I tried not to always be up in my sister's business, but it wasn't easy. She was my other half. So I kept a look out. I knew who her friends were." His brows lowered slightly over dark eyes fringed with pale lashes. "I know you want to talk with your pops on your own, but I say you and me, we pay the baker a little visit tomorrow. Ask her a few questions."

"The bakery's closed," she reminded him.

"I know."

"So you want to go to her house?"

"Yup."

"I thought you were going back to training."

"I am. Will be. But I can spare a few hours in the morning. If you can."

His eyes were eating her up now. There was no other way to describe it. He looked like he wanted to dig around inside her head and consume whatever he found there. Good, bad, right, wrong. It was the strangest thing she'd ever experienced with a man.

"Do you think Deacon and James are going to want to be involved?" she asked.

"Maybe," he said. "Probably. But I think it's best if we do this on our own for now. Three Cavanaugh brothers descending on one already anxious woman . . ."

True. That would be pretty intimidating. "You know, it might be hard to get to her," Grace said. "With what her daddy did, she may not think kindly on any visitors at all."

Cole's lips twitched. Not with humor, but with that singular brand of cocky confidence he wore. "You know me, darlin'. I got my ways. When I want something, I go after it." His eyes dropped to her lips. "By the way, that slice was good. Your soon-to-be husband knows his pizza."

She nearly choked. "What?"

"You heard me," he said, watching her closely.

"Wayne is not my soon-to-be husband. He's not my soon-to-be anything—"

"Did you kiss him?"

"'Course I didn't kiss him." *Wait*. Why was she so vehement about that? She liked Wayne. Wayne was a good man, with solid, real values.

A slow, satisfied smile was Cole's only response.

Nostrils flared, she shook her head at him. "You're insane. You know that?"

"I do. But at least I'm not stupid."

She bristled. "Who are you calling stup—?"

"Don't get all bent out of shape, Doc. I'm talking about Wayne."

"Oh, Wayne is not stupid."

He leaned in, his gaze dropping to her mouth. "Sent you home to another man without givin' you a good, solid kiss good night? Stupid."

"That's called being polite, Cole," she said breathlessly. "Maybe you should try it."

"No, thanks. I'm good."

And with that, he dipped his head and captured her mouth with his.

What he'd meant to do was prove a point. No. What he'd meant to do was play with her a bit. No. That wasn't it either. What he'd meant to do was show her what a man who was interested in a woman . . .

Ah, shit. He didn't know what he was doing.

Her lips were warm and just a little wet as he kissed her, and he wanted to lose himself in them for hours, days—a week. Screw the fight.

The fight.

He growled against her mouth.

The motherfucking fight.

He pulled back. Not all the way, but enough to break their connection, enough so he could breathe on his own and look her in the eyes. She stared at him, heavy lidded, her lips parted—pink. *Oh . . . pink.* He couldn't escape that color. And in this case, he didn't want to.

He forced out a breath. His body felt racked with a desire so intense and unexpected, it nearly made him sick to his stomach. What was he going to do here? He hadn't meant for the silly little nothing peck to turn so epically hot. And from the look on her face, she hadn't expected it either.

Warning. Warning. Back up and pretend that meant absolutely nothing before you blow not only your match next week, but the one reason you came here. The most important reason of all. The truth. Answers to the mystery that is consuming your life.

"Cole . . ." Her voice was so soft, so threaded with need. It made him want to pull her into his arms and remove that tight white dress with his teeth.

But instead he sat back, inhaled sharply, and gave her a wolfish look. "You're welcome."

Her mouth dropped open in shock, and every whisper of desire he'd seen in her eyes a second earlier dissolved. *Real classy, Champ. Yep, you deserve that name tonight.*

"Yes, thank you, Cole," she said with chilly irritation. "Thank you for showing me what a true asshole is."

Ouch. And yet he forced a shrug. "Come on now. I just felt you deserved to get kissed tonight."

"Deserved?" she repeated frigidly, one brow arched.

"You know, because the Rev was probably too timid or gassed up with all that pizza he ate. I wanted to set things right."

For exactly thirty seconds—he counted—she stared at him. Probably trying to figure out what rock he'd crawled out from under and when. He could tell her. The River Black one-screen movie theater, 2002. It had fucked him up something awful. Made him distrusting and an eternal pessimist. Made him turn away from anything good—anything pure he desired. Because he didn't deserve it.

Just like he hadn't deserved that kiss.

She stood up, smoothed her dress. "You are too kind, Cole." Sarcasm bled from her words.

"No problem." It was best she know it now. Know who she was dealing with, and it wasn't no small-town heart-of-gold reverend.

"But I won't be requiring your 'help.'" She used

those air quotes when she said the last word. "Ever again."

He should've felt relieved. "You mad or something?"

She didn't answer him. She was confused by him. And pissed. "I'm going to bed. You can get yourself there, right?"

" 'Course. Almost healed." Ready to get back to his reality. No stolen kisses under the moonlight with green-eyed girls.

She nodded stiffly and turned to walk away.

"Hey, Doc?" he called after her.

She stopped, and with forced patience turned around and glared at him. "What?"

He had it. Sarcasm, innuendo, all that on the tip of his tongue. That was the easy stuff. It cleared the room and made women like the one standing before him refuse to speak to him ever again. But Grace was different. Maybe she deserved better. She hadn't asked him for anything. Just given.

"Thank you," he said at last.

Her lips thinned and she let out a frustrated breath. "Stop messing with me, Cole. It's not okay."

His gut tightened. "I'm not." Not right now. "Swear."

She didn't say anything, just crossed her arms over her chest.

"Thank you for having me here. Taking care of

me. Feeding me." His lips curled into a half smile he knew would be unwelcome. "Letting me kiss you."

"Oh my God, Cole—" she started exasperatedly.

"Working with me to find the truth. It ain't easy, and I know that. I ain't easy. I come with a shitload of dirty, banged-up luggage." He released a breath, all serious now. "But I appreciate it, okay? I appreciate you."

Confusion blanketed her features. She didn't know what to make of him—of his words.

"Don't be mad," he said.

"You make it hard, Cole."

"Yeah, I know. Hey, and if Rev didn't say it," he added, making sure to keep his gaze above the neck this time, "you look beautiful tonight."

She sighed. "Thank you."

"Smokin'. Red hot. Eyeball meltin'. And I'm imagining he probably didn't say it." He snorted. "Shit, if the boy can't even get his ass in gear to kiss you good night, then commenting on your hotness would've probably been an impossible feat."

"Oh my God," she uttered, shaking her head, but a smile was touching her lips now. "Good night, Cole."

"Night, Doc."

"And try not to have any more bad dreams," she called, turning around and heading for the house.

"I'll do my best," he called back.

He watched her walk away, that white dress hugging every inch of her like a second skin. This time, Belle followed. And the stray cat from the night before—the one she'd been desperate to save—darted past. Cole didn't even try to catch it.

Eleven

"Okay, what exactly did the woman say?" Grace asked as she and Cole walked up the driveway toward the well-kept duplex a few streets off Main.

"It was her mother," Cole clarified, the morning sunlight making his blond hair appear almost white. "And when I asked to speak to Natalie, she said Natalie wasn't speaking to or seeing anyone right now."

A groan escaped Grace's throat. "And yet, here we are. Skulking around on private property."

"We ain't skulking, Doc. We have a purpose."

"And what is that? Breaking and entering? Again?"

"You're never going to let me forget that, are you?"

"Probably not."

Cole stopped near the garage and turned to face her. Except for the jeans and boots, he looked nothing like River Black, Texas, in the morning. Tattoos peeking out of the white T-shirt and black leather jacket and that nearly skull-shaved blond head. Nope. He looked like he was from a town called Wicked and it was somewhere around midnight. As he stared down at her, he made her forget to breathe—made her remember the kiss he'd planted on her lips last night. A kiss she'd sworn meant nothing to either of them. Couldn't mean anything.

"Do you really accept it when someone gives you a no for an answer?" he asked, his black eyes searching hers.

Grace's entire face furrowed. "I don't even know how to answer that."

"You gotta push, Grace. If you want something done, you gotta make it happen. No matter what the roadblock."

"I believe that's how you ended up with a restraining order." Nope, not going to let him forget it.

He shrugged, his expression supercilious. "Well, I don't have one anymore, now do I?"

Heat surged into her cheeks.

"She could know something, Doc, okay?" he continued, undaunted. "If she was hanging around Cass, she could know something—could have seen something. You want the truth, right?"

"Of course I do," she insisted.

"We could always bag this and go see your daddy," he suggested.

Her eyes narrowed. "I'm just saying that this could be dangerous."

He looked at her like she was crazy. Like she would never be in danger if she was with him. Or maybe that's just how he made her feel.

"Her father—"

"Is behind bars," he said. "He can't get to her or us."

"Unless he's warned her not to talk to us," she put in. "To you, Cavanaugh brother."

"Let's not put the cart before the horse, all right?" He inhaled deeply, then groaned. "Damn. You smell that?"

She did. It had been wafting her way ever since they hit the garage. Sugar and butter under heat. "Cookies?"

"Oh yeah," he murmured, as if talking to a lover. "I know that smell. From the bakery." He waggled his eyebrows. "Let's go 'round back. Follow our noses. She's home and she's doing what she does best."

"I can't get arrested today," Grace told him as they walked. "I have a neutering at ten."

"Awww, poor guy."

She shook her head, grinned. No matter what the consequences, Cole would always be on the side of the wild and unchecked. It was his side.

"Hurry up, Doc. My stomach's grumbling."

"You're crazy if you think she's going to speak to us, much less offer you a cookie."

"We'll see," he replied, a grin in his voice.

He was moving well now, barely a hint of the sprain in his ankle. Whether he healed quickly or just refused the pain, she wouldn't know. But she was guessing it was the latter. She tended to think Cole Cavanaugh refused to acknowledge pain in all areas of his life.

They were no sooner around the side of the house than a woman in a pale blue dress and white apron opened the screen door and stepped out onto the small porch. She was petite, about Grace's height, and very well put together. Her short blond hair was perfectly combed and her makeup looked flawless. Because their fathers were friends, Grace had seen Natalie Palmer on occasion around town. More so when they were younger. But she wondered if the woman would recognize her.

"You're on private property," she announced, her dark eyes moving from Grace to Cole.

"Just following that incredible smell," Cole told her in that effortlessly charming way of his. "Been trying to find you for days, girl. You know, after you ran out on me."

Natalie looked startled. "You have me confused with someone else. I suggest you go and find her."

He stuck out his hand. "I'm Cole Cavanaugh."

She looked at the hand, then back up at the man. "I know who you are."

Grace stayed where she was, a few feet back from the porch steps. She wondered if this had been a truly stupid move on their part. Would Natalie call the police? Would she go inside and grab a shotgun?

"Then you know," Cole continued, undaunted, "that I'm the one who's been buying up all those ginger snaps at the bakery last few weeks."

It was as if the breeze that had just wafted past stole the woman's sour mood. Even those dark brown eyes softened a hair. "No. I didn't know that." A hint of a smile touched her lips. "But I always wondered who it was. We never had any going into the noon hour. Plenty of customers want to tan your hide."

Cole laughed, a rich baritone that caressed Grace's skin. "It'd be worth it. Best cookies in the world. You should open a bakery in New York City."

A slow, shy smile crept over her face. "They're not *that* good."

"They're perfection." He leaned against the door frame, crossed his arms over his broad chest. "Now, would you be thinking me rude if I got down on my knees and begged for one of whatever you got cooking inside that house?"

As Natalie thought this over, her eyes moving

over his leather jacket, Grace just stared. It was like watching a master at work, and she felt both impressed and horrified at his skill.

"Oh, all right," Natalie finally said. "Stay where you are."

"You kidding?" Cole returned. "I'll be right here. Panting."

Cheeks flushed, she turned away and went into the house. As soon as the screen door slammed, Grace turned on Cole.

"Cookies? Are you serious?"

"Yes. Relax."

"Don't tell me to relax. I thought we were here to talk about—"

She never got to finish her sentence. The screen door creaked open once again and this time Natalie Palmer had a plate of cookies in her hands. She offered it to Cole, who took two.

"Good God, woman," he said after taking a bite. "Pure bliss. Call me selfish, but you need to get back to work."

Natalie blanched. "I don't know . . . Too many people coming in and asking questions . . ." She trailed off.

"It must be hard," Grace said.

It was as if Natalie Palmer had just realized there was someone else in her backyard besides the tatted-up Cavanaugh brother. Her eyes darkened with hostility as she turned them on Grace. "It is.

For my whole family. But especially my father. He's a good man. No matter what anyone else believes. There was a mistake . . . a misunderstanding . . ."

Wow. She was sticking up for the man—calling his assault on Sheridan O'Neil a misunderstanding. Talk about delusion. Or insane family loyalty.

Grace's heart stilled in her chest. Was she doing the same thing? Living in a delusion about her dad and what he did and didn't know about Cass Cavanaugh's disappearance?

God, she hoped not.

"I'm Grace," she told the woman. "Our fathers used to be best friends."

Something flickered in Natalie's gaze. Interest. Curiosity? "You're Sheriff Hunter's girl. I know."

Grace nodded. "That's right."

"You didn't go to school with any of us, though, did you?"

"No. After my mom died, I went away to school."

Natalie seemed to consider this as she turned back to Cole and offered him another cookie. "That must've been lonely."

"It was," Grace acknowledged, surprised at the woman's quick empathy. "I missed home and didn't have many friends." But there were good things too. She didn't have to smell her mother's perfume, sit in her chair, cook at her stove.

"Sounds terrible," Cole piped in, pulling Grace from her thoughts. "Aren't friends in the girl world like . . . everything?"

Natalie's lips twitched. "Sometimes."

"Like my sister, Cass, and her friend Mac." He took a bite of cookie. "Always together."

Grace watched Natalie carefully, and to her surprise the woman's face softened. "She was a nice person. Your sister."

"And a friend?" Cole pressed, his tone taking on a hint of seriousness now. "You two ever hang out together?"

"Not really. But she always said hi to me."

Cole nodded. "You ever see her with any . . . male friends? I always wondered about that, being her brother and all."

Natalie looked momentarily startled, even glanced at the screen door. "Oh, I don't remember anything like that. Not specifically. I remember seeing her with Mac, mostly. And of course, you all."

He eyed her closely, but his voice was real gentle when he pressed, "Are you sure, Natalie?"

"I said I don't remember it," she snapped. Then inhaled deeply. "Here." She handed him the plate. "Take this. It's old and has a chip in it. Enjoy the cookies. I need to be getting back to my work."

"'Course," he said. "Thank you kindly, Natalie."

"Hopefully things will be set to rights and I'll be back at the bakery soon." She gave Grace a clipped nod and disappeared into the house.

Holding the plate as if it held the crown jewels,

Cole headed down the porch steps and along the side of the house.

"Well, that was a bust," Grace said as she fell into step beside him.

"At least we got a few answers," he said.

"A few answers? We got no answers."

"She believes her father's innocent. That's something to consider."

"Of course she does. What daughter wouldn't?" She felt his eyes on her, but she stared straight ahead at his truck. "We came here wanting information on the boy. Sweet. She gave us nothing."

"It's one avenue, Grace. There are more."

Right. Like Palmer. Like her dad. And she was going to have to face that fact. She was going to have to question him for real.

"I'd better get going," she said when they reached his truck.

He hesitated, his eyes on her. "Can I drive you over to the clinic?"

"Thanks, but I think I'm going to walk. It's a gorgeous day." *And I need some time to think. About how I'm going to talk to my dad. About you.*

He nodded, ran a hand through his cropped hair. "Listen, once again, I appreciate all you did for me. Putting up with me."

"And once again, it wasn't easy." She smiled.

He returned it, nodded. "So I'll be back tomorrow afternoon. Can we get together again? Make a new plan?"

"Sounds good." Why was her heart feeling so heavy? It was like a weight was resting on it.

"Here." He handed her the plate of cookies.

"No, these are yours. And you worked damn hard to get them."

He laughed. "I'm in training, remember? I've already had two too many. You enjoy them."

She watched him walk around the truck.

"See you, Doc," he called.

"See you," she offered back, then started down the street toward the clinic. Despite the hot day, she barely felt the sun on her skin. She actually felt strangely cold. She hadn't wanted to say good-bye to Cole Cavanaugh. He was brash and overly charming and sometimes arrogant, but he was also soulful and surprising. Something was happening with her. It had started last night, with that kiss. The kiss she hadn't been able to get out of her head. The kiss that had made it very difficult to fall asleep.

As the truck moved past her and Cole gave her a wave, a quiet thrill went through her. Thing was, she didn't want to pretend that what she was feeling wasn't real. But she couldn't allow herself to get involved with Cole Cavanaugh. Not any more than she already was. It was dangerous. She glanced down at the cookies. She didn't want to see her dad today, didn't want to question him—not yet. But she knew she had to give Cole something when she saw him tomorrow.

Maybe the dad she could see and question was Natalie's.

"You haven't spoken to me in weeks, and now you walk around this house ignoring me."

Blue poured himself a cup of coffee, sweetened with a few spoons of sugar, then turned to regard his mother. "I'm not ignoring you."

Just didn't have anything to say. Anything that didn't deserve a mouthful of soap. And he was way too old for that now.

Closing the refrigerator door, Elena sighed. "Fine, then. Treating me like a . . ." She didn't finish. Just started laying out all the fixings for a salad on the counter.

"Like a what, Mom?" Blue inquired, taking a healthy gulp of his coffee. "Like a person who can't be trusted?"

Her jaw tightened as she snapped the end off a carrot. "I deserve that."

Blue pushed away from the counter. He wasn't going to stand there and have this conversation. Not now. Maybe not ever. He could barely look at the woman who'd lied to his face every day of his life. Who pretended that Everett Cavanaugh was just her employer, when in reality the man was her lover. And his father.

His lip curled. "I have work to do," he said, gulping down the rest of the coffee. The burning liquid scorched his throat.

"You always have work to do," she returned.

"Yeah, well, this place needs runnin'." He stalked past her.

"This place needs to know happiness again," she uttered softly.

But Blue heard her. *Happiness,* he mused blackly, heading for the front door. He couldn't even imagine what that was. What it looked like. If he'd thought he'd experienced it before, he now questioned it. Shit, he questioned everything.

Well, everything but *her.* His Cowgirl. She was the constant. The one person unblemished by the Triple C's past.

He pulled his cell phone from his back pocket as he exited the house and made his way down to the barn. And when he saw she'd texted him, he felt his lungs relax. He could expel and take in air once again. He could allow himself to feel.

Hard day?

He smiled at that.

How'd you know?

☺

He smiled at that too. Then started typing. Behind him and beside him, horses nickered in their stalls.

*Part of me says leave this place and never
come back. It'll drag you down. Its ugly
memories will never give you a day's peace.
But the other part says this ranch is yours.
Fight for it. Take it. Claim it.*

Granted, he hadn't told Cowgirl everything that
had been going on—and no details. They didn't do
details. But she knew enough. Ranch owner had
passed on and left his place to his four children.
Four. And Blue was messed up about it. Had a father, but now that father was gone. Mother had
lied to him. Where did he belong?

Yep. She knew enough.

What does your heart say, Cowboy?

Shoot, his heart was pained one moment, split
in two the next—then running a race inside his
chest. The latter happened every time he heard
from her.

*It says, meet Cowgirl. Face to face. Eyes to
eyes.*

Lips to lips?

His gut clenched. Hell, yeah. She had no idea
how his nights were spent. Where he went in his
mind. How his hand was just trying to keep up.

Before he could type anything, she wrote to him again.

> I wish that could happen. I want to see you more than anything. But my life's too up in the air right now. I need to feel stable, settled.

> *I got stable and settled right here.*

> Don't tempt me.

> *If I had a place for you to come, a place where you felt safe and settled—would you?*

He was talking rashly, impetuously, but he meant it. He needed to see her, have her close. With what was coming—the choices and decisions that needed to be made . . .

> Maybe.

A few yards away, a couple of ranch hands were riding toward the barn. Blue knew he had only a few seconds of privacy.

> *I gotta go, Cowgirl. Think about what I said. What I'm offering.*

He shoved his phone into the back pocket of his

jeans without waiting for a response, a sign-off, and went to get his horse saddled. If he could allow himself to believe it, take it, there might just be a sunrise in his future. *Damn* . . . He'd missed the hopeful, peaceful, new light of day.

Twelve

Grace checked her phone again. She'd rescheduled two clients. They hadn't been all that happy about it, but she'd promised them a substantial discount for the trouble. She glanced up and watched her father's best friend walk into the jail's small visitors' room. He was wearing a navy blue jumpsuit and sporting a pair of tarnished handcuffs. A cold shiver moved up her spine. She hoped the trouble was worth it.

"Dr. Hunter," he crooned, taking the seat opposite her, the only thing separating them, a metal table. "What are you doin' here, girl? Your daddy send you?"

She shook her head.

"Naw," he said. "That boy is in a jail cell of his own, now, ain't he?"

Grace didn't respond. She'd never realized before how deep and menacing his voice was.

"I got the cookies you brought," he continued. "Well, two of them anyway. A guard ate the rest. 'Checking 'em for weapons,' he said." Caleb snorted. "That son of bitch."

So that's what had done it, she mused. The cookies. Natalie's cookies. They'd lured him out of his cell to talk to her. Wasn't about her dad. She wondered if Caleb even gave a shit about her dad. As far as she knew, he'd barely visited the man in the past year.

"I just saw your daughter," she managed. "We talked a bit. Then she gave us the cookies when we left."

His eyes lit for about a half second. Then he sneered. "Us? Who's us?"

Oh, shit. Stupid . . .

"Wasn't one of them Cavanaughs, was it? They tried to get in here to see me." He grunted. "Can't stand how those bastards are ripping apart my family."

"Well, maybe they didn't appreciate how you treated James's fiancée, Sheridan O'Neil."

His eyes roamed over her face until they lifted to catch her gaze. "That girl is a right bitch."

Heat slammed her in the chest. No, she clearly did not know Caleb Palmer. "Listen," she began. "I wanted to talk to you about my dad. I was visiting him yesterday—"

"Good man," he interrupted. "Such a good man."

"He says the same about you."

His mouth curved up at the corners, and his eyes softened.

"He says a lot of things," she continued. "Things that don't really make sense to me."

"What kind of things?" Wariness was back in his eyes.

"Things about the past. His friendship with you. Something you may have taken blame for?" When he didn't react, she leaned forward an inch or two, her disgust overpowering her fear. "You told James Cavanaugh you knew who killed his sister."

"Did I?" he said smoothly. "Don't remember that. Must be all the choking he did. Squeezed the memories right out of my mind."

That's how a Cavanaugh male reacts when scum like you is threatening his woman. God, just thinking about how Caleb had crashed Mac and Deacon's wedding to get close enough to Sheridan O'Neil to . . . to what? Hurt her? Kill her?

Like Cass?

Her breath caught in her chest, and she stared hard at the man in front of her. "What happened to that girl?" she demanded. "Where you a part of it? Was my father?"

A slow, evil smile curved his lips. "Like I said, your father's a right good man." He stood up. "Tell him I said hello when you see him next."

As he walked away, headed for the guard who had been watching them the whole time, Grace felt her skin crawl. She knew without a doubt that he'd hurt Sheridan, and would probably do it again if given the chance. But she honestly didn't know if he had any information about Cass's disappearance. He seemed mentally unstable, and she prayed he never got back out on the streets.

Her phone buzzed, and she glanced down at the readout. It was Rudy. She had thirty minutes to her next patient. What was she going to tell Cole? What was she going to offer him in exchange for him going with her to see her father? Because he wouldn't let up. And if she was in his shoes, she wouldn't either.

At least she'd have a day to think about it, to plan, she thought as she headed out of the jail into the warm and welcoming sunshine.

For thirty minutes, Cole had been asking himself just what the hell he was thinking. Acting like a teenage boy with a crush? *Turn around, get back in your truck, and head to Deac's place. The chopper's waiting on you.* And yet he pulled back the door of the veterinary office and went inside. He hadn't been in there since his law-breaking days, but it was pretty much the same except for the sounds of a few dogs barking. He spotted a young Latino man sitting behind the reception desk, and he headed that way.

"Afternoon," the man called out. "Can I help you?"

Cole glanced around. "The Doc in?"

"She is, but she's finishing up with a patient. If you'd like to wait . . . or is there something I can help you with?"

"You know how long she might be?"

"I don't." The young man set down the paperwork he'd been engrossed in and gave Cole his full attention. And by full attention, Cole guessed the guy was getting pretty suspicious. After all, he had no dog, no cat. Just a need to see the Doc.

"We're friends," Cole said, as if that explained everything.

Clearly it didn't, because the guy's brown eyes narrowed. "If you'd like to leave her a message, I'd be happy to give—"

His words were cut off abruptly by a door flinging open. Two chocolate Labs burst out, straining their leashes as they whined and whined.

"Just keep them away from the oranges," Grace told the older man who was holding the leashes. "Otherwise I'll be seeing you once a week."

The man nodded in understanding. "It's our neighbor's tree, Dr. Hunter. They won't stop going over there. They eat them off the ground."

"Maybe it's time to invest in a fence," Grace said, patting his shoulder a couple of times. "Or maybe don't let them get out without being on a leash."

"This is Texas," the man continued.

"I know, I know. But it's you who has to clean up that mess."

She glanced up then and spotted him. Her eyes softened and a slow, genuine smile touched her lips. "Hi."

He touched his hat the way he'd seen Deac and James do a hundred times. "Doc." He'd never been much for manners, but there were some people in this world who made you want to be better, do better.

"What are you . . . ?" she started, then turned back to the older man. "Mr. Kennedy, Rudy here will set you up with meds and some food. The girls need food that's gentle on their stomachs for a few days. And I'll call you later to check up on them."

He nodded. "Thanks, Dr. Hunter. And I'll keep 'em away from the neighbor's."

As he and the two Labs headed over to the reception desk, Grace motioned for Cole to follow her. He knew instantly where they were going and suppressed the urge to grin.

Scene of the crime.

"So, that's Rudy," Cole said once they were inside her office.

Grace closed the door and headed for her desk. "That's Rudy."

"How long's he been working here?"

"A couple of months," she answered tentatively. "Why are you here and not in Austin?" A sudden anxious look crossed her features. "Is it your ankle? Are you in pain again?"

"Nah. Ankle's good."

"Oh." She sat on the edge of her desk. She looked a little distracted. "So what's going on?"

That squeeze thing was happening in his chest again. He'd had it on the way over, and the night before when he'd been an ass and kissed the woman who'd been nothing but kind and cool to him. And now he was going to act like Ass Number Two.

"I stopped by because . . . well . . ." He looked up, connected with her confused, concerned gaze. "I wanted to ask you something."

"Okay."

"How do you feel about helicopters?"

Her brows knit together. He was so damn smooth—kind of like a piece of barbed wire.

"I want you to come with me, Grace," he managed to shove out.

Her lips parted. "To Austin?"

"Yes."

A pink blush touched her cheeks. "Oh. Why?"

Well, that wasn't the reaction he'd expected. Just a yes or no—or more likely, no fuckin' way. "You ever seen a fight? Boxing match? Anything like that?"

"I saw a boxing match. But on TV."

"And did you keep watching or did you turn it off?" he probed.

"Cole, I'm confused. And normally I'm a pretty bright person, so the fact that I'm not picking up on what's happening here is sort of freaking me—"

Ah, damn. He wasn't good at circling the wagons. "I'm into you," he ground out. "All right? There it is. I'm sayin' it plain. And when I thought about going to Austin for the night, I thought it'd be nice to have you with me. I know this isn't a good idea, with what you and I are trying to do. You for your dad and me for Cass. Better if I don't come over to your house ever again. We do our investigating over a table at the diner." He exhaled heavily. He sounded like an idiot. "I have training later this afternoon—you don't have to go to that, of course—but we could go to dinner. Austin is a great town—don't know if you've been there. Deac said we could have full use of the chopper, so I can run you home later."

She said nothing. Just stared at him. Something was going on behind her eyes, though. He could tell. Large, intelligent emeralds flickering in the light of her office lamps.

Then she crossed her arms over her chest and lifted her chin. "No pizza."

"Come again?" he asked, confused and feeling like a twelve-year-old boy.

She laughed. "Just thinking we could have something else besides pizza. Just a joke."

Understanding dawned, and it felt pretty great. He grinned wide. "I have a great place to take you."

"And I'd like to go to your training too, if that's okay."

"Really?"

She nodded.

"It's pretty violent. Might make you either sick to your stomach or completely repelled by me."

She laughed again. "Maybe. But you know, I see blood, guts, and broken bones all the time."

It felt like a balloon was being blown up inside his chest. So full, so tight. Warm too. It was the strangest sensation he'd ever had. And maybe the most addictive. She wanted to go with him. To dinner. To his training. It was the first time he'd ever asked anyone . . .

"What about your work?" he asked. "I don't want to take you away from anything."

"I'm actually done for the day." She looked down for a second. "I only had a couple of patients. And the few things that need finishing up can be done by my very capable assistant Rudy."

Something pinged in his chest, popped the warm balloon. "Good man."

She looked up, caught his gaze. "Rudy? Yes, he is."

"Just like the Rev."

She looked at him strangely. "Suppose so."

"You lookin' for good, Doc?" He couldn't stop the words from spilling out of his mouth. Because he needed to know. And maybe she needed to know he wasn't that—*good*. Didn't know how to be. Didn't want to be. Didn't deserve to be.

She didn't answer him at first. Just got up, walked around her desk, tidied up a few things. Then she took off her lab coat and hung it on the back of her chair. She was wearing jeans and a black T-shirt that was fitted real nice to her upper body. She grabbed her purse and came to stand beside him.

Her eyes twinkled and her lips curved into a happy smile. "You'll have me back by midnight?"

He grinned. "Okay, Cinderella." Then he offered her his arm. Shoot, if he was going to attempt the manners thing, might as well go balls out.

Thirteen

Grace had the reputation of a woman with an iron stomach. Nothing turned her. She could go on boats, fly for hours in constant turbulence, put animals' guts back inside their bodies and sew them up. And yet the second she walked into the gym and saw a man in the ring hit another man so hard one of his teeth flew out of his mouth and landed not six inches from her shoe, she nearly lost it.

Yep. Horrific.

Is this what I came to see? she'd asked herself. And worse, when Cole came out would he be doing the dental work?

"You all right, little lady?"

Grace glanced up and shook off her thoughts. She was sitting on a bench beside Cole's trainer. His name was Matty, and she was pretty sure—

after the introduction they'd had and her bout with tooth-flying nausea—he didn't like her.

"Fine, thanks," she said, forcing a smile.

Matty inhaled deeply, looked around the decent-sized gym with its two sparring rings, a large, square-matted area that was dotted with punching bags, and a full weight room. "I got to tell you, I don't think you should be here."

Yep, the man didn't like her.

"You and Cole an item?" he asked before she had a chance to respond.

"No. Just friends." The ancient trainer didn't need to know anything that Grace herself didn't know. What she and Cole were.

The man's eyes narrowed. "Here's the deal. My fighter needs to be one hundred and fifty percent focused next week."

"I'm sure he will be."

"You don't know much about this sport, do you?" he asked.

"Practically nothing," she admitted.

"If a fighter doesn't want to get killed in the ring, he needs total focus. If he wants to win, he eats right, drinks nothing that'll cloud his head and make him slow. And he doesn't partake in bedroom activities—if you get my meaning."

Oh, she got it all right. Just didn't want to hear anything more about it. "Isn't this a conversation you should be having with your fighter?" she asked.

"I have."

"Then why bring it to me? Like I said, we're friends."

"I wish I could believe you," he said, studying her. "But this is too important. When Cole brings a pretty gal in here to watch him train . . ."

"I'm sure he's brought plenty of gals in here," Grace said with a laugh.

Matty's brow lifted. "See, that's the thing. He hasn't. In fact, he's never brought anyone to a training session or a match."

You could've knocked her over with a light wind. "Never?"

He shook his head real slow. "He's been smart, savvy, and focused until now."

"He's not unfocused," she assured him, then felt absolutely ridiculous for doing so. "For heaven's sake, it's one practice, one gal."

But Matty was unconvinced. Looked at the ring and just kept shaking his head. "I don't like it. Don't like it at all. And if he gets knocked out today, I'm blaming you."

Grace stared at him, stunned. "Oh, come on." This was insane. What had started off as a date was slowly turning into a badly scripted drama.

"Stop talking to her, Matty," Cole called out good-naturedly.

Grace glanced up, spotted him coming out of the bathroom and getting into the ring. As if on cue, and completely without her consent, the breath inside her lungs promptly evacuated.

"I ain't doing nothing," the man said.

"Better not," Cole said, dancing in place, releasing some of the tension in his muscles.

Damn, that had to be a lot of tension, she mused as she took him in. He was shirtless—of course—his muscles bunching and flexing beneath tanned skin sharp with tattoos. She'd heard someone refer to tattoos on a man's body as "tongue tracers" once. She'd thought that sounded bizarre and kind of gross. Now she could very well imagine it. Imagine herself—her tongue—running over each design, the salty taste of his skin turning her mind to . . .

She scrubbed a hand over her face, hoping to erase the inappropriate thoughts she was entertaining.

It didn't work.

Another man bent down and slipped through the ropes, entering the ring. Cole hadn't introduced her to him, but he'd talked about him on the flight there. He was Cole's sparring partner, Reg. Reg wasn't as broad as Cole, but he stood maybe three inches taller and he looked mean. 'Course, so did Cole. In fact, they both looked like bulls ready to strike. As Grace watched, the pair talked back and forth, then gave each other a double fist pump.

"You ready, ladies?" Matty drawled. "Or would you like a cup of tea first?"

Grace turned and shot the man some serious

shade. Nothing she hated more than using women or girls as a metaphor for frailty. But Matty paid her no mind. He was up, off the bench, and making his way ringside.

"His weakness is his ankle," Matty told Reg.

Why would he tell him that? Grace thought with stunned disgust. Did the trainer want Cole to injure himself further? Why on earth? She was about to stand up and head over and ask him when first contact between the UFC fighters was made.

Reg to Cole. A kick to the face. Grasping the bench to steady herself, Grace gasped, actually feeling the impact. Blood trickled from Cole's left nostril. As she watched, he lapped at it with his tongue, then grinned. Matty glanced back over his shoulder and gave her the stink eye. She glowered at him. This was not her doing. For God's sake! But in seconds there was another strike to Cole's face. This time by the man's fist. Then another to his gut.

TV boxing hadn't prepared her for the intensity of mixed martial arts. Or the scent of sweat and blood and tension and hunger in the air. Why had she come here exactly? To see him at work? See his skill? See him beat someone to a pulp? And why had he wanted her to be here? Did he want her to see what he'd devoted his life to? What kind of man he was?

And what kind is that, Grace?

"Shit," she hissed under her breath as Reg went for another fist to the face.

But this time Cole reacted. Fast and furious, he hit back hard, three punches, sending the man flying back on his ass. Grace's hands came together in an almost-clap, but she caught herself. Good thing too, because Reg had recovered and was sending the heel of his foot directly at Cole's hurt ankle. The groan/curse that erupted from him nearly had her turning away—would've had her walking away if she could get out of the gym unnoticed. She hated seeing him in pain. And yet she had a sneaking suspicion that, somehow, he reveled in it.

In seconds, everything changed. On a dime. It was like a light switch had turned on and Cole went to work. Forget the nose. Forget the ankle. He was landing punch after punch into Reg's face. It looked like the man was turning from side to side. One, two, three, four, then a knee to the ribs and one last uppercut to the jaw.

Poor Reg cried out, backed up quickly into the corner. He cursed and spit blood onto the mat. Grace assumed the fight was over, but Cole had other ideas. Breathing heavy, eyes blacker than a starless night, he paced a circle in one corner. He looked different, different from the Cole she knew. He looked like a machine. All emotion turned off.

Matty was calling time as he climbed into the ring. He went for Reg, tossed the man's arm over his shoulder, and helped him down. Reg was bleeding badly. His nose was surely broken. Was this normal? Did they always train to this degree for UFC? That seemed insane.

As Matty moved past her carrying out Cole's sparring partner, a smile curved his lips. "Forget what I said, little lady. You're welcome here anytime."

Revulsion pulsed through her. Was the trainer truly under the impression that her presence had caused his fighter to amp up his game? Her eyes shifted to Cole. He was still breathing heavy, still pacing, still bleeding from the nose. But his eyes were pinned to hers. They weren't as dark and bottomless as they'd been a moment before. But they held fire and pain and a hunger for something she didn't understand. Something she wasn't sure she wanted to understand. He had wanted her to see him like this. Out for blood. Feral. But why?

And why—after everything she knew and had experienced with him—had she accepted?

Diary of Cassandra Cavanaugh

May 7, 2002

Dear Diary,

He called! Sweet called me tonight! Maybe he's called before but I didn't pick up the phone so maybe he hung up or something. Anyway, I answered the phone tonight and there he was. He told me he's not in River Black. I guess something happened back home where he's from and he had to go there. But he'll be back tomorrow.

I'm so excited!!!

And I'm so crazy!!!

I thought he didn't like me anymore. But that's not true. It was just some emergency. He wouldn't tell me what it was but he whispered a lot when we talked, so it must be a secret.

We made plans to meet at Carl's tomorrow night. I don't know how I'm going to sneak out but I just have to. I wish I could tell Mac. It'd be nice to have help from a friend. But I think she'll say he's too old. That it's not right.

*Maybe she'd even tell on me. That's not going
to happen.*
Anyway!
Soooooo happy,

Cass

Fourteen

"It ain't fancy," Cole said, inhaling the killer scent of fire-roasted chiles and hand-rolled tortillas. "But the food is the best I've ever had."

He watched as Grace took in the Tex-Mex hole-in-the-wall he loved so much. Her sharp green eyes moving from the small bar, wet with margaritas and tequila shots, to the large outdoor eating area with picnic tables and a full moon rising up above.

"If you don't like it, we can go somewhere else," Cole backtracked, not wanting her to feel uncomfortable. It wasn't suit and tie. Not like somewhere Deac would take Mac. But it was him. And maybe he wanted her to see something of him that wasn't knuckles on bone or blood spatter on canvas.

"No, I love it," she said quickly, turning to look at him. Her eyes were warm, just like her smile. "I'm not really a fancy kind of girl."

His gut tightened. "That right?"

She nodded. "And Tex-Mex is my favorite. The spicier the better." She grinned wide.

His brows went up and maybe other parts of him did too. Good God, this woman continually surprised him. And to surprise himself, he reached out and took her hand. Her breath caught and she bit her lower lip. It was a bold move, and maybe slightly stupid when he was trying to resist the call of Grace Hunter. But it felt right in the moment. She felt right.

He led her to a small table in one corner of the outdoor space. It was pretty busy in Fausto's. Lots of singles, families reconnecting after a long day. Everyone relaxed and having a good time. He needed that tonight.

"*Hola*, Cole!" the owner called out.

Cole waved back. "Good to see you, Fausto."

"Nice eye shadow," the man's wife, Maria, called from behind the bar. "You in training again?"

He grinned. "Yup."

"No chips and queso for that boy!" Maria called out.

Cole laughed.

"They know you here," Grace said as they sat down.

Cole nodded. "I come in pretty often. Lunch, dinner . . ."

"You don't cook?"

"No. But even if I did, I don't have an oven."

She picked up her menu. "Wait. How is that possible?"

"I live in a hotel."

Cole waited for her to look stunned or appalled or any of the other things that showed up on a person's face when he told them about his living situation. But there was none of that. She just nodded, then took a sip of water.

"I'm sure you're traveling a lot," she said.

"Yes. Exactly."

"And deciding on a home base isn't practical right now," she concluded.

He just stared at her. Like he was staring at an alien. Or an angel. Did this woman actually get him? Shit, no one got him. He counted on no one getting him.

"Drinks?"

Cole turned to see Maria sidling up to their table. She was dressed in a jean skirt and a bright orange blouse. Her long black hair was neatly braided and her face was free of makeup except for her standard red lipstick.

"What are you doing?" he chided. "No one waits on tables here. Least of all you." His eyes narrowed. "What's happenin'? Why ain't you making us order up at the bar like everyone else?"

Maria's eyes flickered in Grace's direction. "I don't think your date here needs to know how ungrateful you can be, Cole Cavanaugh."

"Oh, I'm not his date," Grace said quickly and with a soft laugh. "It's . . . a friend . . . thing."

A friend thing. It was easy how she just tossed that out. Like she believed it. Needed to believe it.

Maria's eyebrows lifted. "Trust me, honey. If he brought you here, it's a date."

Grace turned three shades of red and looked down at her menu.

"Can we get some chips and salsa?" Cole asked brusquely. The woman was crossing all kinds of boundaries.

"She can," Maria put in. "But you'll have chicken, beans, and a large ice water."

"Come on, Maria," he chided. "I need some heat."

Maria turned and winked at Grace. "See what I'm talking about?"

Still three shades of red, Grace shook her head, then started to laugh. "Am I going to be setting myself up for sexual innuendo if I also ask for something with heat?"

Maria burst out laughing. She looked back at Cole. "Oh yeah. Good for you."

"I'm sorry about this," Cole told Grace.

"It's fine," she assured him.

"Can I get you something to drink, honey?" Maria asked her. "We have the best margaritas in Texas."

Grace turned to Cole. "If I get one of these Texas Proud Margaritas and you are stuck with ice water, will that end our friendship?"

Even though Cole knew she was kidding around, playing with him—and damn cute-like too—something inside him kicked. Hard and right to the ribs. She kept calling him her friend. Even knowing how he felt. He'd been honest when he'd told her that he was into her. True fact. Attracted. Would certainly like to try some more kissing. But what he hadn't known then was how she made him feel outside of the heat and curiosity. She was fun to be around. Calm and easygoing. Nice. She made him feel comfortable. That, way more than the desire, was cause for concern.

He shook his head. "Have that drink, Doc. Everyone should experience Maria's margarita once in their life."

"Let's hope it ain't only once," Maria put in, grinning. "And what about food, darlin'?"

Grace closed her menu and sat up a little straighter. She seemed to have recovered from the embarrassment. "I love cheese and I love spicy, and I love surprises."

"Oh, I'm going to make sure you get something special," Maria said, then leaned down and whispered in Cole's ear, *"No estropees esto."*

Then she was gone and headed for the kitchen. Cole stared after her for a second, then shook his head and returned to his date/friend. Who knew? Not him.

"Can you tell me what she said?" Grace asked, her green eyes glittering with humor. "Or is it a secret?"

"Oh, she was just lecturing me. In Spanish." *No estropees esto.* Don't screw this up. He shrugged. "Thinks she's my fairy godmother or something."

"Your fairy godmother?" Grace repeated, cocking her head to one side and grinning.

He laughed, scrubbed a hand over his bruised face. "I had a twin sister. She watched a lot of Disney movies. That's the only excuse I got."

She lifted both hands. "I'm not judging. But I do recall you mentioning Cinderella to me not long ago as well."

He sighed as drinks were placed in front of them. "Fine. Maybe I liked those movies too. The *Beast* one is good. And maybe the one about the boy who didn't want to grow up."

"*Peter Pan*," she supplied.

He pointed at her. "You liked them too."

She grinned and took a sip of her margarita. "Oh dear baby Jesus."

"What?" he asked, concerned.

"This is so good," she said on a groan.

A wide grin spread on Cole's face. "Maria will now be your friend for life, you know that?"

"I'm cool with that."

"And she'll want to see you in here at least once a month."

"Is that the standard request?" she asked, laughing. "For any friends you bring here?"

"I wouldn't know."

Her expression turned thoughtful as she took

another sip of her drink. "So, I take it you haven't brought many dates here."

The question was unexpected, and Cole's face grew serious. He felt it happen, felt it take over his body. "Does it matter?" He would've really appreciated a beer right about now. Or maybe something stronger. But after his show in the ring, the last thing he wanted was to lose any more control.

"No," she said. "Just curious."

He hated ice water. At least she could've thrown in a couple of limes. "The truth is, Doc, I have fun. Enjoy myself. But I don't bring anyone into my life. Not in any meaningful way, so to speak."

Her eyes caught and held his. "But you brought me in."

He stared at her. His chest was filling up with air and heat.

"Can I ask why?" she said. "Matty told me you've never had anyone at your training sessions. Now you say you've never brought anyone here."

"I told you, Doc. I'm into you." His words sounded forced.

She shook her head. "I sat there and watched you get hit over and over. I watched you make another human being bleed."

"That's the game—"

"Did you want me to know how dangerous you are? Or can be?" she asked. "Did you invite me here to turn me off?"

"What?"

"So I wouldn't like you back?"

It was as though she could see inside him. "That sounds crazy."

"It sure does," she agreed. "But you kind of believe you are crazy, don't you, Cole?"

Cole had never felt his chest as tight as it was now. He was all for being honest. But there was something about being honest with Grace Hunter that scared the ever-lovin' shit out of him. Why had he invited her? He'd wanted to be around her. Wanted to get to know her better. Wanted her to get to know him.

All of him.

"Hot plates!" Maria called, zooming in tableside, putting an end to their very intense discussion. Efficiently, she placed some plain chicken, unsalted beans, and a small cup of mild salsa in front of Cole, then a plate of heaven in front of Grace.

He just stared at the steaming plate across from him. "You are one heartless woman, Maria," he ground out, picking up his fork.

The woman laughed, but her eyes were settled on Grace. "Don't you listen to him, honey. And don't you cave when he begs you to share. He's in training and that makes him irrational and cranky as fire ants." She winked. "You enjoy."

"Thank you," Grace said, her voice a little quieter than before. She was thinking. "It looks amazing." Before picking up her fork, she felt Cole's eyes on her and glanced up. "What's wrong?"

"That Evil Stepmother gave you my usual."

One brow lifted. "Really? What is it?"

"Chiles rellenos with green sauce." He heard the yearning in his voice. It competed with the Spanish guitar music being pumped out from the speaker above them.

She laughed. It was good to hear. And her eyes unclouded too. "Poor Cole."

"That's right." He pouted.

"How strict is this training diet you're on?" She cut off a section of chile with her fork.

Cole's mouth instantly watered. "What are you doin'?"

She stabbed the piece, then lifted it to his mouth. "A taste isn't going to get you in trouble."

"Oh, Doc, that's exactly how I get into trouble. One. Little. Taste."

He hadn't meant the words to come out sounding all sexed up, but clearly they had. Her cheeks were turning pink right before his eyes. Then he grinned and put his mouth on the fork. A groan escaped him as he tasted New Mexican chiles, cheese, tortilla, a hard bite of spice.

"Good?" she asked.

His eyes captured hers. "I'll never have enough," he answered.

Her breath caught in her throat, and she pulled

the fork back, cut a bite for herself. She licked her lips in anticipation. He watched her eat. He watched her as if they were the only two people in the place. Melted cheese, tortilla, and he knew she was catching the heat each time she took a bite. It was hypnotic. She had a pretty mouth, straight white teeth, pink tongue.

He shifted in his chair. Below his waist, shit was happening. Shit he didn't want, and certainly didn't need. Not now. He grabbed his water and downed the whole thing.

For a few seconds they ate in silence, listening to the guitar music and the other patrons talking and laughing. Then she said, "Can I ask you something, Cole?"

"'Course."

Her eyes lifted to meet his. "What is it about fighting that draws you in? Makes you feel that this is your passion, or pride, or your life's work?"

With what was happening inside and outside of his clothes, the question stalled him a bit. He had to put his head on straight. No one had ever asked him anything like that. Not in the thoughtful, interested way she just had.

"I don't know if I see it as a passion of mine as much as a compulsion," he answered.

"You feel like you have to do it?"

"I do."

"Or what?"

He shook his head. "What do you mean?"

"Well, what happens if you don't do it?" she pressed.

He'd never thought about it. But now that he did, the idea made his insides quake. It felt like a tsunami churning his guts. If he didn't fight . . . what? What would he be or do? How would he keep himself sane? How would he keep making amends to Cass? He had become a fighter to shut down the weakness that used to live inside him. The weak boy who couldn't protect his sister when she'd needed him most.

"I can't imagine my life without the ring," he said, then stuffed a piece of chicken in his mouth. He knew it wasn't dry, but it tasted that way anyway. His gaze drew up, locked with hers. "Why did you become a vet?"

For a moment or two, she just looked at him. Maybe deciding if she was going to push him for more of an answer to her question or not. But then she started eating again. "Do you believe in reincarnation?"

He shrugged, wondering where they were headed. "I don't think so."

"I didn't either," she said, then slipped a piece of chile between her lips.

Spicy green sauce and Grace Hunter's pink mouth . . . trouble.

"I was a very cynical child," she said, dabbing

her mouth with the paper napkin. "Everything had to be proven, you know? Until my mom died anyway." She placed her fork down on her plate and picked up her drink. "At the funeral this very dear friend of my mother's told me that my mom would always be with me. Of course, I told her that was impossible. That I didn't believe in those stupid ideas at the grand age of ten."

When she smiled, he did too.

"I was really laying it on thick—I was so angry and confused. Anyway, just as I was going off on how impossible that idea was, a dark brown cat came out from behind one of the gravestones. Right hind leg clearly broken. And it hobbled over to me. Lay down next to me. It . . . wouldn't leave me. After the service, my dad and I took her to the vet. The doctor said another day and he wouldn't have been able to save her leg." She was thoughtful for a second, maybe remembering the cat; then she inhaled deeply. "That day I'd started out feeling hopeless and angry, but by sunset I felt like maybe I had a purpose. I could save someone's life, even if I couldn't save my mother's."

He knew exactly what she was saying. He didn't have a cat appear to him, but that's what fighting had done for him. Given him a purpose. Granted him forgiveness.

"Do you believe that cat was your mother?" he asked.

She shrugged, smiled softly. "I don't know."

"I guess death can make us believe some strange shit, do some strange things."

"Like fight an endless battle?"

It was as if the sounds around them had been ripped away and only stark, awful silence remained. Grace was staring at him as she took a sip of her margarita.

"We're talking about Cass now, right?" he asked, breaking the quiet. "Not the ring?"

She shrugged.

"That what you think I'm doing? Fighting an endless battle over what happened to her?"

She sighed. "I don't know. It popped into my head. I'm not trying to peg you or fix you or diagnose you—" She started to laugh.

Cole did too. Couldn't help himself. "Well, that's good to know."

"I'm just trying to understand you. Not all that smart of a thing to do or say between two people with conflicting goals. But there it is."

For several long seconds, Cole just stared at her. Such a pretty woman, lips and cheeks flush from the heat of the chiles, and eyes that didn't judge him, only questioned him. Wanted to know him, she'd said. Why'd she have to be the way she was? All the things she was? Making him think and question? And wonder . . .

He glanced down at his phone. "It's nearly eight thirty."

"Is our coach about to turn into a pumpkin?" She gave him a gentle smile.

Damn, he didn't want the night to end. "Helicopter's scheduled for nine."

She placed her napkin on her nearly empty plate. "We should get going, then."

"Yeah." He pulled out his wallet. Maybe he could hurt his ankle again. Stay in the pink room for a few more days.

"Hey," she whispered.

He looked up.

"Smile, Cole Cavanaugh," she said brightly. "The sunshine is good for your teeth."

He took her hand and led her out of the restaurant.

Sun's gone to bed, Doc. And goddamn, if we could get out of here unscathed, that's exactly where I'd love to take you.

Grace felt good. Warm. Relaxed. No doubt courtesy of the margarita and the man sitting next to her in his beautifully restored blue Mustang convertible. But when he pulled up near the airstrip where they'd landed earlier and killed the engine, her heady buzz turned into a solid, deep ache. She didn't want to go. Her body had started to grow accustomed to him. This fighter. This man who was both simple and complex, kind and brutal.

Her eyes caught on the Cavanaugh helicopter

in the distance. The Long Horn shone blue under the stark moonlight. It was waiting. Ready to take her back home where she belonged. Ready to take her back to reality. But she didn't want to go. Back to the investigation. To all she hadn't told Cole. To the pull of the truth—to her father's potential past deeds.

But she had to. She had started to open her door when she felt Cole's hand on hers. It was strong and warm, and she gave it a gentle squeeze as she turned around to face him one last time.

He looked contemplative. A struggle was going on behind those dark eyes of his. "You okay?" she asked.

"I want to go with you. Walk you to your door and all that."

A soft smile touched her lips. "That's very nice, but you have an all-day training session tomorrow." *And I have a meeting with Sheriff Hunter.* "I think you should go home."

"I don't have a home."

He sounded so comically down that she laughed. "Yes, you do."

"It's a hotel."

"And probably a beautiful one. Go get a good night's sleep, Cole."

He released her hand, drove his fingers through his hair, and growled.

"What?" she asked.

"I'm not tired."

Her lips twitched. He sounded like a petulant boy. A boy with lots of muscle and a significant amount of body art. For a few seconds she allowed herself to wonder just how much body art he had. And if there were any pieces he kept hidden.

"If I fly with you," he said, pulling her from her thoughts, "I'll sleep on the way back."

Tempting. So tempting. "You're not thinking."

His eyes darkened. "You're right."

Tendrils of delicious heat snaked through her. And without forethought, she reached out and touched the bruising under his left eye. "You need to rest. We want to make sure this doesn't happen again."

Something flashed in his eyes. Something she'd never seen before. A thread of vulnerability, maybe. Then he turned his head and kissed the inside of her wrist. Grace gasped. Not loudly, just a quick intake of breath, but Cole heard it and his nostrils flared. *Friend.* Why was she calling him that? That's not what they were—what they were becoming.

It's because that's all you should be. Where can this possibly go? He's shown you what he is. An endless battle . . . a scarred brother. A man who sees no end to his struggle. And then there's you . . . secretive . . . scared . . . keeping so much from him.

She let her fingers move gently over his face to his jaw, then to his neck. The look he gave her turned her blood to lava. Hot, hungry, uneasy. A warning that if she kept touching him he was going to touch her right back.

Heat pooled low in her belly as she stared at him. It was as if she had no control of her actions when she was this close to him. As if her mind had been severed from her heart and instincts. Her hand stole around his neck and she leaned in and kissed the bruise beneath his eye. When he groaned, she did too. Panic and lust were flaring within her. She wanted him, wanted to be touched by him—wanted to kiss him—but she was also scared of going down this road again. Another charming bad boy who lived in the moment—or in Cole's case, the past—and didn't want to look to the future. But what was that future? For either of them? She eased back a few inches, gazed into those intense black eyes. *You started this, Grace. You touched him first. You kissed him . . .*

And then his mouth was on hers and she forgot the world outside even existed. Forgot anything she'd thought before or questioned. His kiss took her, captured her, owned her. Made her knees weak. He tasted like the sugary mint Maria had placed on the table with a copy of his credit card receipt. It was delicious. He was delicious. She wanted to crawl up on his lap, wrap her legs around his waist, run her hands into his hair. And before she could stop herself, think, or reason, she did exactly that.

Forget that the car wasn't all that big or accommodating. That the top wasn't down and her head skimmed the cloth. Forget that the chopper waited in the distance, and Cole needed rest and recovery. His hands were on her waist, his fingers dipping underneath her tank top. Her belly twisted with need and her underwear was wet. She'd never felt this charged in her life and kissing him just wasn't enough.

His hands skimmed up her lower back, the rough pads of his fingers against her hot skin. She groaned against his mouth, drove her tongue inside and tasted him. More sweet. More mint.

His fingers worked the clasp of her bra, unhooking it in seconds. She was free, her nipples beading—waiting for his touch. But instead his hands continued up her back to her shoulders. And then he was taking off her shirt. She only noticed because he tore his mouth away.

His incredible mouth. God, his lips were full and talented. He wasn't one of those eager guys who slobbered all over you or tried to ram their tongue down your throat. Oh, he wanted her. She could feel the hard length of him every time she pressed herself closer. Impressive. She moaned at just the thought—the hope. God, could they do it in this car?

Her shirt was off. Bra too. She was naked from the waist up and loving the cool air on her skin.

"Oh, Doc," he uttered on a near growl, pressing her back ever so gently against his steering wheel. His eyes—black and glittering with possessive hunger—raked over her. "You are one gorgeous woman."

Breathing heavily, Grace watched him. Watched as his hands went to her neck, his fingers tracing over the two cords of muscle, then over her collarbone. She wanted to scream at him: *Hurry up! Damn you. Hurry up! I'm going crazy here. I want more. You. Hands on my breasts. Mouth on my nipples. I want to be licked and bitten and—*

Her thoughts disintegrated as he filled his hands with her, as he massaged her breasts, first gently, lovingly, then hungrily, his teeth gritted. Her sex felt heavy, tight, so wet. She felt madness touch her mind. Never in her life had she wanted anything more than this man.

"Look at you," he ground out, his fingers finding her nipples. He pinched them both lightly.

Grace cried out, ground her hips against his erection.

"You've changed my mind about pink, Doc," he said, tugging, pulling, circling.

"Oh God!" This was insane. She was going to lose her mind. Or come. Right here in this car.

Her hands went to the button of his jeans. She needed him, needed to feel him.

But he stopped her. Left one of her breasts and

gripped her hand instead. Their eyes met and locked.

"What's wrong?" she asked through labored breaths. "You don't want me to touch you?"

"Fuck, yes, I want you to touch me," he said through tightly clenched teeth.

"Then let me."

"No. Fuck." He took her hand and guided it to her breast. The breast he'd abandoned. "I can't. Nothing. Not until this fight is over."

Realization dawned, and she shook her head. "Then let's stop. Both of us. I can't—"

"Oh, yes, you can," he said fiercely. "And you will." He flipped the button of her jeans and rammed the zipper down. "Touch your breasts, Grace. Show me what you like. Show me what my mouth should be doing."

Confusion warred with inexplicable desire inside her. She hated that he could have nothing and she was going to have everything. But he was determined and she was too far gone to fight. As she squeezed her breasts all the way to the nipples, flicking them, rolling them, Cole dipped into her underwear and found her slick, wet folds. His nostrils flared and he cursed.

"Someday," he began in a guttural tone, "this hot, wet pussy will be mine. Jeans off. Underwear torn by my teeth and discarded on the floor." His fingers sank between her lips and found her swollen clit. "First I'll lick you. Every inch. Until my throat ain't dry anymore. Then I'll ease my tongue up inside you until you cry out."

Grace was one fully charged power line ready to explode. His fingers played her clit as she played her nipples. Flicking, circling, pinching. Cream trickled from her sex onto the backs of Cole's fingers.

His eyes turned so black the pupils disappeared. "I have to know. What I'm missing. No, that's not right. What I can look forward to. My prize when I win." His thumb rested on her clit as he slid two fingers inside her. "Ah . . . fuck, Grace. Oh, baby. How'd you get so hot?"

But Grace couldn't speak. Not in any real way. Moans, cries, hopes to give more, take, yes . . . Her body was his. He was pumping inside her, his thumb pressing against her clit. The build was glorious and greedy, and she came, pumping her hips, forgetting her breasts, just gripping on to whatever she could for support. Her cries were loud and shocking, and didn't recede until he eased his fingers from her and pulled her tight against his body.

They remained that way, heavy breaths in a car with fogged-up windows, for long seconds.

"Stay," he uttered. "No, fuck, don't stay."

She laughed softly. Or she thought she did.

"I want you. If you stay . . ."

"Don't, Cole," she said. If he really asked her,

she would. She was in no position to refuse him anything. Her body was still screaming. Not for another release, but for him. Inside her. All night long. "Can't. Belle and work."

"Okay, then I'm going with you."

She shook her head. "No. Please." She pushed off him, into her seat. She zipped and buttoned, then reached for her bra and tank. "You need to focus. You need rest." As she yanked her tank back on, she swore she heard him mutter, "I need you," but she refused to acknowledge it. "And maybe we need to get our bearings. That was . . . intense." She scrambled out of the car.

Cole was beside her in an instant. His jaw was as tight as the rest of him. But he took her hand as he walked her over to Deacon's helicopter. He gave a *Hi* sign to the pilot, then helped Grace inside. She strapped herself in, feeling hot and uncomfortable.

He stepped back, his eyes locked with hers. He looked ready to explode, and she wondered if abstaining included not touching himself. She thought that was probably the case. The more sexually frustrated, the better.

She wasn't sure how she felt about that.

"Say hi to Belle for me," he said.

"I will. In the morning. She's staying at my neighbor's. Rest, okay?"

His nod was clipped. "Safe flight."

He backed away, nearly to the edge of the grass.

As she rose into the air, and as he grew smaller and smaller, she settled into her seat and thought about closing her eyes for a while. But something was buzzing in her purse. She opened it, pulled out her phone, and started checking her e-mails and texts. Her heart leapt when she saw a text from him. He'd sent it just seconds after takeoff.

Let me know when you're home safe. —C

Fifteen

Cole exited the helicopter, bags in hand, and strode across the back lawn of Redemption Ranch. It had been two days since he'd been back to River Black, but, for some reason he refused to acknowledge, it felt closer to a month.

With a quick glance at the nearly finished house his brother and Mac were now occupying, he headed for his truck. Though he appreciated Deacon's generosity with the rides to and from Austin, he wasn't in the mood to chat. He wanted to check on Grace and Belle. See if they had missed him. See if one smiled and the other howled when he opened the door.

Christ, he was an idiot.

"Welcome back, brother."

"Shit," Cole ground out.

"What's that?" Deacon called from the porch.

He headed down the steps and over to where Cole had parked his truck.

"Just sayin' thanks for the lift." Cole tossed his bags in the back of the truck.

"Anytime," he said, leaning back against the driver's-side door. "You know you could always get one of your own. I know you got plenty of cash socked away in a mattress or two somewhere."

"Sure. But where would I park it?"

"Backyard works for me." Deacon shrugged. "Wouldn't hurt you to set down some roots, Cole."

"Actually, I think it would," Cole returned. "Excuse me. Someplace to be."

Deacon pushed away from the door. "A house here in River Black could be interesting."

"Come on, big brother," Cole said, climbing into the cab. He started her up and rolled down the window. "You know that'll never be my way. Can't be. Home was always where Cass was. When she went . . ." He shook his head. "Hotel is just fine."

Deacon stared at him for a second. "I didn't know that about you. Didn't know that's why you lived like you do."

"We all have our scars from that battle," Cole said. "The shit we feel we'll never get over or forgive ourselves for."

"Wasn't your fault, Cole."

"Sure." He nodded. "Wasn't yours either."

A look of mutual understanding passed between them. Then Deacon crossed his arms over his chest. "Does Dr. Hunter know that you're never going to settle down in this town?"

Just the sound of her name sent a rush of adrenaline-laced desire through him. "She knows I live in a hotel. And she's pretty accepting of it."

"You need to tell her," Deacon countered. "It's not fair, Cole."

Cole dropped back against the seat and sighed. "I know."

Deacon glanced at the house, then back again. "Listen, she's visiting her dad right now. She called a little while ago, invited us all to come by and talk with Sheriff Hunter."

"Well, let's go. What're you waiting around for?"

"I think you should go. I think I want to know what happened to Cass so badly it aches inside me. But I'm not willing to bombard an old man who's sick in the head to get it." He blew out a breath. "Go gently. See what you can find out."

Cole studied his elder brother. The guy used to be consumed with hate and vengeance. But things had changed in the past couple of months. Mac had changed him. Like Sheridan had changed James. Cole used to think that was a bad thing. A loss of control. But he wondered what that kind of peace felt like.

He shoved the truck in reverse, then called out the window at Deacon, "I'll let you know."

Deacon nodded. "And hey—don't forget Palmer's arraignment tomorrow morning."

As if I could, Cole thought as he gave his brother a casual wave, then backed up and headed out of the driveway. But first he was going to see Grace.

"Jell-O is a very underrated dessert," Grace stated. "I especially like the orange. It's got just the right amount of tang. I appreciate you giving it to me."

There was no reply. Which was becoming standard with her father over the past two days. She sat in a chair beside his bed while Belle lay at the foot. Grace had been forced to hoist the basset hound up there because her howling in protest had brought the nurses rushing into the room.

"So what are you watching, Dad?"

"*Project Runway,*" he said, not taking his eyes off the screen.

"Do you watch it often?"

"It's my favorite. All them pretty gals. Reminds me of Millie."

Grace's heart squeezed with the mention of her mother.

"You didn't know my wife," her father continued. "But she sure liked to dress up fine. Beautiful woman." He stuck his chin out. "I wish she was here with me now."

Me too.

"But she's gone. Dead. So many people dead."

Who was he talking about? People here in the care facility? People he used to know?

Cass?

And where were the Cavanaugh brothers? Where was Cole? She'd called several hours ago, invited them. She'd thought they'd be here in a heartbeat. Questions in hand. It hadn't been an easy decision to allow them access to her dad, but she knew they weren't going to stop pushing,

She closed her eyes briefly. How far was *she* going to push? How hard?

"Who besides Millie passed on, Dad?" she asked. Her heart was beating so fast she could feel nothing else.

"Look at that," he exclaimed, pointing at the TV. "A dress made out of flowers. How'd they do that?"

"I don't know," she said.

"Millie would've loved a dress made of flowers."

It was too much. It hurt too badly. He was fading away from her. Dementia had him in its grip. "I think Grace would love a dress made of flowers too. Pink flowers."

He turned then and looked at her. "Who's Grace?"

Tears pricked Grace's eyes. *No. Oh, no, no, no.* "She's your daughter."

"I don't have a daughter. Me and Millie never were fortunate enough." He turned back to the television. "That Heidi Klum couldn't hold a candle to my Millie."

Pain lanced through Grace. She couldn't hold on to herself any longer. She stood up and walked out of the room. She heard the *click-clack* of Belle's toenails behind her, but she didn't stop until she was out the door and in the sunshine. She put on Belle's leash, tears streaming down her face, and was about to run to the car when she ran into a man instead.

"Grace?"

It was Cole. Finally Cole.

"What happened?" he asked, his voice edged with concern. "Christ, baby. What happened? Are you okay?"

She couldn't speak. She just clung to him and cried.

Sixteen

He made her leave her car there. Said they'd come back to get it. Then tucked her into his side in the truck and took her home. Once there, he made her some weak coffee and brought it out to her on the porch. She was sitting on the weathered bench, and her hands shook around the cup.

She hadn't said a thing to him. On the drive. Or when she got home. About what had happened inside the senior care center. But he was worried. Seeing her pale and in pain made him crazy.

He came around to face her and squatted down on his haunches. "Talk to me."

When she didn't answer, he touched her chin gently and lifted her eyes to his. But once she looked up at him, the floodgates opened and tears streamed down her cheeks.

"Grace . . ."

She shook her head. "I went to see Palmer."

His gut tightened. "What? When? Dammit, Grace. He's a monster. He could've . . ." He looked away, then back again.

"I tried to get something from him. Anything. To admit he knew something about Cass. But"—her voice broke—"he acted like he had no idea what I was talking about."

"I wish you hadn't gone there," Cole said. "Alone."

"All he wanted to talk about was my dad. What a good guy he is." Her eyes lifted to meet his. "I failed, Cole. I wanted to get you something from Palmer. Something from my dad. But . . ." She shook her head.

He felt her anger, her frustration. He wanted to take them both away. "What happened?" he asked gently.

"My dad didn't say anything about Palmer or what happened back then," she said with a slight bitter edge to her tone. "He's just getting worse. Further and further away from me . . . from reality."

The pain in her eyes sliced through him. "I don't care about that right now. Any of it. I care about you." And damn if he didn't mean it. He stayed where he was and took her hands in his.

She deflated instantly. "He doesn't know me."

"But that's happened before, right? He's gone in and out."

Her eyes swam with tears. "He doesn't think he

even had a daughter. At all. That he and my mom never had a child."

Cole stared at her, his chest tight. The war inside him was a dark, demented one. On one side he had this woman he was starting to fall for. This woman he cared about more than he should. And she was in pain. Because of the father she loved. On the other side, he had the boy whose twin sister had been ripped from his life. The boy who grew to be a man who constantly fought to keep his soul intact and his ass out of jail. A man who looked at every opponent as the monster who killed his sister.

The man and the boy wanted answers. At all costs.

A light rain began to fall, hitting the stones beyond the porch with a pitter-patter.

"I'm so sorry, Doc," he said softly.

She nodded. "Thank you. And thanks for taking me home and making me coffee. You didn't have to."

He reached up and wiped the tears from her cheeks with his thumb. "What else can I do?"

"Nothing." She was quiet for a moment, then said, "It was just a shock, you know?"

"Sure."

"You think you'll always belong to at least your family. You never think it's possible to belong to no one."

Cole struggled for words. She would belong to

someone. Someday. A good, solid, openhearted man who lived in River Black and wanted nothing more from her than her heart. Christ, she deserved that. She deserved someone honorable.

He sniffed bitterly. *Like the Rev.*

Behind him, the sky broke open and the rain began to fall for real, in thick, hard sheets.

Grace looked past his shoulder and laughed softly. "I swear we attract this weather."

"Living life in the gray," he said. "That's how we do. Sometimes the sunshine is too bright, lights up all the things you don't want to see. Or are afraid to see. You know what I mean?"

She nodded. "Oh boy, do I ever." She took a healthy swallow of her coffee. "I need to get to the clinic. I'm late as it is."

"No you don't."

"I have a patient today. Teeth cleaning on a very ornery golden retriever."

"I called the clinic just now. I told Rudy you weren't feeling well. He said he'd take care of it, reschedule."

Her face darkened and her entire body went rigid. "When did you do that?"

"When I was making the coffee," he explained. His eyes searched hers. "Are you mad?"

"Yes, I'm mad. You don't just take over someone's life like that." Her voice caught and she turned away.

He inched closer to her. "I wasn't trying to take

over, Doc. I swear." Fuck, he'd messed this up. Didn't know how to do this.

"You made a decision for me without even consulting me." She wasn't looking at him. And her voice was warbling again.

"Christ, Doc, you were upset. Cryin'. I thought you needed time or something—"

"That wasn't your place, Cole. You're not my boyfriend. You're not my anything. You're just here to get information."

"Hey." He touched her cheek, turned her to face him.

Her eyes were filled with tears again. "Well, I don't have any. I have nothing—" Her voice broke and she started to cry again. She put her head in her hands and crumpled back down on the chair. "Fuck, I can't believe I don't exist."

Cole stood up and slid one arm under her shoulders and another under her knees. "It's okay," he said, lifting her into his arms. "It's going to be okay, Doc."

He carried her inside the house and into her pink bedroom. He placed her down on the bed, then slipped in beside her. He pulled her close until her cheek rested on her chest, and then he just let her cry it out.

Strangest thing, he thought, staring up at the ceiling, stroking her hair. And probably one of the most striking. He hadn't comforted anyone in a long time. Not since Cass.

*   *   *

When Grace woke, it was near dark. At first, she wasn't sure where she was, what she was lying on, or whose arms she was wrapped in. Then the afternoon came rushing back to claim her, and both pain and heat filled her body.

"Cole?" she whispered.

"I'm here, Doc."

She could feel the vibration of his voice against her cheek. "You didn't have to . . ."

"I know," he said quickly. "Wanted to. That's the thing." His hand moved in circles on her back. "I'm not good at it. Don't know how to do it well. But I want to. A lot."

She knew exactly what he meant. What little experience she'd had with relationships hadn't turned out well. This one, whatever it was, felt good, right. And yet . . . "Does that scare you? How much you want it?"

"Yup."

She smiled softly and nuzzled against him. "Why?"

"Because I'm not made to care for someone."

"And yet you did. You are."

A beat. Then, "Long term."

Grace inhaled deeply. "No one's asking for that."

"Yeah, but they might deserve it. They do deserve it."

It was obvious that he wanted her just as much as she wanted him. Heck, her thigh was resting

across his groin. But she also knew that he was trying to let her know that she deserved someone—
anyone—but him. He thought he wasn't worthy of
her. He thought he wasn't worthy, period. How did
she combat that? How did she convince him that
he was?

You can't, her heart warned her. You can only
accept what's here now. Enjoy what's here now.
And if at some point Cole walks away, then he
does. And life will go on. Rain will still fall. Dogs
and cats and horses will need help. *But maybe, for
the first time, you'll know what love feels like.*

"How did training go?" she asked softly. "Sorry
I didn't ask you before. Did you massacre Reg
again?"

She could almost hear him smile. "Only sparred
with Reg once. It's all he would give me. Seems
I'm borderin' on animal when I'm out there. No
one wants to get too close or go too long."

A little thrill moved through her at his words.
This tender, tatted-up badass. "Matty must be
thankful for that."

"Matty wondered where you were," he said.
"You two have a conversation while I was in the
ring?"

"I think he's under the impression that I bring
out your animal side."

"He'd be right," Cole said darkly.

"Well, I have yet to witness it."

A low growl sounded and Grace felt him move

away from her. In seconds, she was on her back and Cole loomed over her. Her heart started to beat wildly in her chest. She knew they couldn't have sex. Not yet. Not now. She knew he wouldn't allow her to touch him. Not yet. Not now. So when he started unbuttoning her jeans and yanking down the zipper, she knew exactly what she was in for.

"Cole . . ." she started, heat pooling low in her belly.

His eyes glittered like black diamonds, and the shadows caused by the slashes of rain against the window behind her made his expression deliciously fierce.

"I'm hungry, Grace," he said. "I missed lunch."

Her heart jumped in her blood and she couldn't stop the grin that spread across her face. "Poor baby."

He returned her smile, his teeth gleaming white. He started to ease her jeans down over her hips, then yanked them to her ankles and off onto the floor.

Grace fidgeted against the mattress, eager yet frustrated too. "It's not fair. I don't get to touch you. You get nothing—"

"Stop." He pulled his shirt over his head and discarded it, then managed a sort of reverse pushup, so they were nearly nose to nose. "You have no idea the pleasure I get from touching you," he whispered. "Tasting you."

Grace lost her breath.

Until Cole kissed her. Softly, gently.

Then her instinct was to wrap her legs around his waist and hold on tight. Forget the fight. Forget herself. Just exist in a world where Cole Cavanaugh existed inside her. But that couldn't be tonight.

When he pulled away from her, she groaned, missing him instantly. She watched him move down her body, his muscles bunching, the lines and symbols of his tattoos moving as if alive. Until he was between her legs.

As the rain pounded the windows behind her, Cole Cavanaugh nuzzled her sex through the thin cotton of her underwear.

"I want these," he said, giving the fabric a nip. "Want to carry them around in my back pocket so I can smell you all day."

She laughed and groaned simultaneously. "You are completely perverted, Cole Cavanaugh."

"Get used to it," he returned, then suckled her through the fabric.

Grace's hands fisted the sheets as every nerve ending in her body stood at attention. This man drove her to distraction, captivated her. Made her wish there was no world outside these walls and that the rain would never stop.

She felt his fingers on her inner thigh; then he pulled the cotton fabric aside and licked her from entrance to clit. She gasped and her hips jerked up.

"You are the sweetest," he whispered between gentle flicks to her swollen bud.

"Oh God, Cole . . ." She came up on her elbows. She wanted to watch him.

He was so focused, his tongue pressed flat against her sex. Slowly, he moved in circles. Grace could hardly hold her weight. The buildup inside her was quick and almost painful and made her feel frantic. She wanted everything at once. His fingers inside her. His cock inside her. She wanted to flip around to that ridiculous sixty-nine position and suck on him as he was now sucking on her.

And then Cole penetrated her with his tongue. Her head dropped back, and as he pumped inside her she felt the heat fill her, swell within her. She was going to come. She didn't want to. She wanted more of this, of him. But it was too late. Cole drove up inside her and started flicking his tongue deep within her pussy. Grace cried out and bucked against him, letting her body take the orgasm it craved. Never had she felt like this. Never. What would she do if this was it? If this ended? If Cole Cavanaugh never touched her again?

She sat up, sending him back. Her eyes met his as her hand wrapped around the thick shaft straining inside his jeans.

"Hungry?" he asked, his lips glistening with her arousal.

"Starved," she hissed.

She got to stroke him once. Down his shaft. Then Cole's hand covered hers and he shook his head. "Can't." His pupils were dilated and his nostrils flared. "Now I'm going to get the fuck off this bed and you're going to take those panties off, give them to me, then slip your jeans back on and be ready in five minutes."

"Why?" she asked breathlessly.

"We're going to dinner." He pushed himself back and off the bed. "You said you were hungry."

"Not for food." She pouted.

He stood there for a moment looking down at her with jaw tight, muscles blazing, and tattoos so ready to be licked. "Sorry, Doc. That's all I can give you right now."

Seventeen

"How did you get so good at this?" Cole demanded when Grace sent another dart straight into the target.

"Single woman after work at the Bull's Eye," she explained. "Lot of time on my hands."

Cole didn't believe her. "Really."

"Or maybe it was summer camp." She looked confused, then shrugged. "Either way, I'm clearly gifted."

Cole laughed. He was doing a lot of that these days. Didn't go hand in hand with his fists, feet, and fight mentality, but it changed something inside him. Something he'd never known he was missing. He followed her over to the booth she'd claimed earlier and slipped in beside her.

"You know this was the booth you and Rev were sittin' in that night I saw you?" he told her.

"That was clearly not one of my lonely after-work single nights."

She was kidding around, and normally he would've followed her there just as he'd followed her into the booth. But after what they'd shared today—both in her pink bed and out—he just couldn't get there.

He sat back against the fake leather. "Seriously, Doc. What's up with you two?"

Her humor waned. "We're friends," she said evenly.

"Like you and me are friends?" he pressed.

Her cheeks turned pink and she glanced around the room nervously. "I am really thirsty after my incredible win. And hungry too. A ton of calories lost tonight, Cavanaugh."

"Grace—"

"What say we both order turkey burgers and ice water?"

"There a reason why you're avoiding this question? It's real simple. You like him or you don't."

She sighed. "Well, of course I like him. He's a man of the cloth."

"I think that's a Catholic thing."

"Whatever. Do I like him? Yes. Do I go on dates with him sometimes? Yes. He's a good man. Stable. Kind. Wants things I want." She stopped, realizing what she'd said. Maybe hadn't meant to say.

"And what's that?" Cole asked her, feeling every muscle in his body go rigid. "What do you want, Grace?"

Once again she glanced out at the crowd. When she turned back, she put her elbows on the table and let her chin rest on her palms. "I want to be happy. I want to be loved. I want someone to grow old and cranky and sexually bored with."

When that last bit registered, Cole laughed. "You don't want that."

"I actually do. I mean, I'm hoping the bored thing happens when we're both ancient and drooling on the lapels of our housecoats. But I want it. Here in River Black. I didn't get a chance to really set down roots here. I have that chance now."

Cole frowned. River Black. Just like Deac had said. Of course she wanted to stay here, live here. Why wouldn't she? She had a life, work, friends. A home.

You could have those things, a voice whispered in his ear. *Don't have to fight anymore.* No more battles. Only win after win after win—starting with her.

No. That's not in the cards for me. Home and the love of a good woman. *No. I don't get the happy ending, because Cass didn't get one. Period. End of story. Fight. Goes. On.*

"So, you planning on Rev being the one?" he said. "The one who buys you that housecoat and drools beside you?"

The bitter edge in his tone wasn't lost on Grace as he said this. She stared hard at him. "Why are you asking me this? Pressing this? And with so much anger."

"There's no anger," he lied.

"Do you not want me to date Wayne anymore?"

Of course he didn't. He didn't want her anywhere near him, or any man. But how could he ask that? How could he even suggest it? When he was unable—no, unwilling—to give that to her?

"I'm sorry I brought it up," he grumbled, his chest tight. Jaw too. "I'm gonna head up to the bar and put our order in."

"I can do that. Or we can wait for a server."

"This'll be quicker." He slipped out of the booth. "I know how hungry you are." *And I know I need a minute. Get my shit together. Get my head together.* "Turkey burger, right?"

"Yes. With cheese."

"Anything else?"

"Can I have some fries?"

He couldn't stop the words from spilling out of his mouth. "You can have anything you want, Doc."

Her eyes widened and her cheeks flushed. It was all Cole saw before he turned away and headed for the bar. As he maneuvered through the noisy Sunday night crowd, he knew he needed to back off this possessive track he was on with her. She didn't belong to him. Not that she needed to belong to Wayne either.

He groaned. He was hopeless.

His ass started to buzz just as he came up to the bar, and he grabbed his phone out of his pocket. He recognized the number glowing up at him as Deacon's cell.

He stabbed the green call button. "We're having some dinner," he said instead of a hello. "Can I call you back later? Nothing much to report about the visit with Sheriff—"

"Cole!" Deacon broke in harshly. "Oh, fuck . . ."

Just the weight in his brother's voice had his heart dropping into his stones. "Is it James?"

"No. He's fine." There was a heavy exhalation. Then, "It's Caleb Palmer."

Cole's gut started to churn. "He's out, ain't he?"

"Worse."

"Shit. What's worse than that?"

"He's dead."

Grace picked at the cold turkey burger she'd brought from the Bull's Eye to the kitchen of the Triple C. It was the meeting place the brothers had all decided on, since James and Sheridan were staying there and Mac was working there.

Everyone except James was seated around the massive table drinking coffee or beer, supplied by a concerned-looking Elena Perez. Grace didn't know the dark-haired woman all that well. She'd seen her in town a few times. And she knew she was Blue's mother, and about the scandal of Blue being Everett Cavanaugh's son. But Grace had the feeling there was tension in the house around her. The woman was trying real hard to take care of everybody, yet she looked very uncomfortable and self-conscious while doing it.

"He had a heart attack in his cell," Deacon informed them. He had a beer in one hand and was rubbing Mac's shoulders with the other.

"Are they sure?" James countered, his gaze flickering to the table, where Sheridan sat, her face pale.

Cole looked up at him. "What do you mean?"

The man shrugged. "I mean, besides Grace's fruitless conversation with him, did someone else get in there somehow and kill the bastard so he couldn't talk tomorrow?"

"Talk about what?" Grace asked. She still couldn't believe the man she'd sat across from not one day ago was dead.

"Anything he might know about Cass's death," Deacon supplied as Cole gave her a tight smile.

He was sitting across from her, tense but oddly protective. Every time she looked his way, she caught him staring at her.

A plate was set before her. Meat loaf and mashed potatoes. Steamy and making her mouth water. "I can't sit here and watch you eat that cold lump," Elena said. "Please . . ."

"Oh, thank you," Grace stuttered. "You didn't have to—"

"Oh, yes, I did," Elena fired back before returning to the stove.

Grace got the feeling the woman was very pleased to have the entire family there in the kitchen, no matter how on edge she was.

"Well, it seems we're back to square one," James said. "Unless . . ." He looked at Grace questioningly. "Anything from your dad—"

"No," Cole said quickly, almost snappishly. "Nothing to report."

"What's wrong with you?" James ground out.

Cole's eyes were on Grace. "Nothing. Just pissed about Palmer, is all."

"Can't say I'm all that broken up about it," Sheridan put in. Though her face was pale, her voice was strong, resolute.

"I hear they're having the funeral tomorrow night," Mac said, sipping her beer.

"Who the hell's gonna go to that?" James said with a snort of disgust.

"I say we all go," came a new voice.

They all looked up. Blue Cavanaugh was standing in the doorway. He wore his cowboy duds, caked with both dust and mud. His handsome face was tan and sharp angled, making his vivid blue eyes stand out. One thing was true, Grace mused: the Cavanaugh brothers—though very different in their appearances—were all gorgeous as hell.

He shrugged, didn't seem bothered by their

hard, curious stares. "The Cavanaugh family should put in an appearance, is all I'm saying."

"Why?" Cole asked tightly. "That asshole tried to kill one of our own."

Grace glanced at Sheridan. The woman nodded. "Can't argue with that logic. I won't be paying him any respects. But I will be sleeping better tonight."

"Oh, baby," James said with a look of love so deep and true the whole room felt it.

"I think everyone can make that decision for themselves," Deacon put in. "But there might be something to learn there." He shrugged. "Palmer's wife and daughter might not be so closed off in that environment. Grief has a way of getting people to drop their defenses."

Grace's stomach started to churn and she pushed her plate away a few inches. Granted, she'd come to despise Caleb Palmer and wanted him to never see the light of day. But the way Deacon was talking, the way Blue was talking, and James—it was disrespectful and inappropriate, and not something she wanted to be a part of. It had been one hell of a day and she was beat.

As if sensing her mood, Cole pushed back his chair. "It's time we went home. Doc?"

Every member of the Cavanaugh clan stopped and turned to look at him. For a moment, Grace didn't understand what the problem was. But then she got it. Those expressions—especially the ones on his brothers' faces—told the whole tale. Hotel-living player and fighter had used the words "we" and "home." She wondered if they'd ever heard that out of him before. She guessed not. No doubt it was, even now, echoing through their minds like a puzzle they weren't sure how to piece together.

But Cole wasn't one to stick around and explain. In fact, he didn't acknowledge any of them. Not until he came around the table and reached for her hand. Not until she gave it to him.

"Grace has had a long day," he said, then released a weighty breath. "Shit, we all have. Boy, things keep changing." He looked at each one of them in turn. Even Blue, who was still camped out in the doorway. "But at some point this merry-go-round is going to creak to a stop and each one of us is going to have to decide to stay on or get off. Whether the truth is revealed or stays buried with Cass."

No one said a word as he led Grace out of the room and out of the house.

Diary of Cassandra Cavanaugh

May 9, 2002

Dear Diary,

Mom almost found out about my sneaking out at night to meet Sweet. She was coming downstairs for something from the kitchen and I was coming in the back door. She thought I was a wild animal.

She locked the door!!

I spent the rest of the night in the barn. All the animals had gas and I wanted to cry. But at least I was with Sweet beforehand. I think he's going to ask me to be his girlfriend. We sure kiss enough.

Well, someone is still following us. I know it. I can feeeeeel it. It freaks me out. 'Course, I still can't tell Mac about it. I just don't want to get her in trouble or me in trouble. But guess what? Someone else is helping me. I didn't think I could trust anyone with my secret. But sometimes you have to trust. Anyway, now I have a lookout when me and Sweet are together.

Maybe we'll get married someday.

Mr. and Mrs. Felthouse.

Mr. and Mrs. Sweet.
Don't know which I like best.
Gotta go to school. I'm sooooo tired.
Zzzzzzz,

Cass

Eighteen

"What are you doing in there?" Grace called through the door.

Cole glanced around the bathroom. Was this bullshit? Or had he actually pulled something off here? He didn't know. He was going on instinct, not experience.

"Keep your underwear on, woman," he called out. "Oh, wait. It's still in my pocket."

"Not funny."

He grinned. "C'mon now. It's a little funny."

"Seriously, what's happening in th—"

Cole cut off her words by opening the door. She was right there, waiting, hovering, her brow furrowed.

"Going through my medicine cabinet, Cole?" she asked wryly.

His grin widened. "Honey, you're going to feel

real bad for sayin' that in a second. Or real good, depending on how you see things."

He stepped aside so she could see what he meant, and her mouth promptly dropped open. *That's right, Doc.* Slowly, she walked inside the dimly lit bathroom. Took in the bubbles, the steaming water, the two cherry-scented candles he'd found under the sink. Granted, it wasn't the Ritz or anything, but it was nice.

"You drew me a bath," she whispered, her back to him.

Ah, Christ, Cole thought, cringing. Was it his imagination or did she sound on the verge of tears again? Why the hell did he try things he knew nothing about? Maybe she hated baths. Maybe sitting in a vat of hot water disgusted her. Shit, who knew? Whatever it was, he had to get out of it. He could say it was for him . . .

"You drew me a bath," she repeated. Then she turned around to face him.

Relief rushed through Cole. No tears, though she looked a little weary. And from the day she'd had, who could blame her? But in her green eyes true appreciation glowed. She didn't just like the bath setup, she was slightly awed by it.

"I thought you could use some pampering," he said.

"I could," she agreed, her gaze moving over his face until she connected with his eyes again. "I really could. This was so thoughtful of you."

Okay. Why'd she sound so surprised? He wasn't a total cretin. Granted, he'd always used the bathtub in his hotel as a superlarge ice bucket for parties after his fights. But this was much better. And he was glad he hadn't screwed it up.

"It was nothing," he said, his voice rough. "So I'll step out. Give you some time, and maybe give Belle some time. I think she's pissed at me. Thinks I'm neglecting her."

"No." The single word snagged Cole's attention.

"I'm serious, Grace. She gives me the evil eye every time I walk past her. 'Course that could just be the basset hound thing—"

"I meant no to your leaving," she said, her eyes soft.

Oh. Damn.

Not leaving the bathroom. Her in the tub. "Oh, Doc. I can't get in the water with you." Just saying the words made his chest tight and his lower half start having ideas.

"I know," she said. "But if you can handle it, I'd love to have you stay in here with me. Talk. Hang out."

Cruel and inhuman punishment is what that sounded like. He laughed. He didn't know if he could handle it. But denying this woman anything was just a superpower he lacked. "You sure? You don't want to relax or de-stress or whatever?"

Her brows lifted and she smiled. "Did you just say de-stress?"

He shrugged. "I know things, Doc. Hear things. Read crappy magazines when I'm waiting on my takeout."

She laughed. "So you'll stay?"

He sighed. "If you'll explain things to Belle."

"Don't worry. She's very understanding." With deft hands, she started to undress. "I'll make sure she gets a few cookies in her system before I tell her."

Cole sat down on the floor, his back against the wall. Best not to get too close. It was strange. Both from her angle and his. In his life, he'd seen women naked more than he cared to admit, but he felt inexplicably shy about seeing Grace. Like he didn't deserve it, or some shit like that. But that was right. That was his whole goddamn issue. What he deserved. What he didn't. The list got longer every day.

When he heard water splashing, he looked up. Seated inside the tub, surrounded by a sea of pale pink bubbles, was the most beautiful woman he'd ever seen. Truly, she was a stunner, her creamy skin glowing in the candlelight, her eyes on him. They were so bright, so green, and so confused and curious.

"You looked away when I got undressed," she stated.

Ah, hell. Did she have to? Have to make him explain? Always said whatever was on her mind. He liked that about her. But sorta hated it too. A grin split his features.

"Believe me, Doc," he said finally. "I'm as confused by it as you. It wasn't for lack of wanting to—I can tell you that." He stretched his legs out, crossed his arms over his chest. "Water okay? Not too hot?"

Her eyes softened and she shook her head. "You keep doing these nice things for me and we're going to have trouble when the time comes to say good-bye."

Her words were sharp and unexpected. Cut into him. Deep. "Who says we're saying good-bye?"

Her lips curved into a soft, sad smile. "I know who you are, Cole. And who you're not. It's part of your charm." Her smile widened. "And I know why you came into my life in the first place. What you want from me."

"Hell, woman. I don't even know what I want from you. Well, that's not true." His head dropped back against the cool tiled wall. "But how I got here isn't as important as why I'm sticking around, is it?"

Her brows lifted. "Why are you?"

"I told you before." His eyes drank her in but left him with a deep thirst for more. "I'm into you."

She smiled shyly.

"Will you come to my fight?" he asked impulsively. "Be there on the sidelines?"

Her smile upgraded to a full-blown grin. "Cheer for you when you win?"

He nodded. "Pick me up off the ground if I lose."

She gave him a look that said, *Are you crazy?* "You're not going to lose."

"I've never beaten this guy, Doc." His voice was unexpectedly rough. Maybe even held a trace of longing, if he was going to admit it.

Her eyebrows went up and down real fast. "That's what's going to make it so great."

He laughed at her silly face. "Why do you have so much faith in me?"

Her eyes glimmered and she gave him one helluva megawatt smile. "Because I'm into you too."

He'd heard people say—on TV, in movies, books, even from guys at the gym—that really liking someone can make your heart shift inside your chest. To make room. For the other person's heart. He'd always laughed off shit like that. Someone's heart inside him, cuddling up close to his ticker. Shoot . . . there were days he was pretty sure he didn't even have one. That the muscle had stopped working the day Cass was taken, was yanked out and buried when she was found dead.

Then this girl, this woman sitting in a sea of bubbles, had to go and tell him she liked him, that she believed in him. Making his heart pull a Grinch. Not only was it still in there and beating away. It had swelled.

His eyes held her tight. "Can I stay the night?"

She nodded.

"In your pink room?" He grinned. "Your pink bed?"

She nodded again.

"I don't think I can touch you." He groaned with the thought. "Though, Christ Almighty, I want to. But I don't think I can stay sane if I do. You understand."

Her lips formed the sweetest smile. "We'll sleep."

He released a breath. "I know you've never slept with a guy until me. But I want you to know I've never slept with a girl until you."

Her entire face lit up. "Really?"

He nodded. "Never even thought about it."

"Oh, that makes me happy, Cole," she said, relaxing back against the tub. "Boy, this feels so good."

"I'm glad, Doc. Real glad." He dropped back against the wall, and for a little while they enjoyed a shared silence.

*   *   *

Cowgirl.

I'm here.

Have you thought any more about it?

I'm always thinking about it.

Then let's just jump. Time is precious. Who knows what tomorrow will bring?

What happened?

Blue glanced up. Following the afternoon rain, the clouds had moved on and a sky glittering with stars had emerged. The land he loved so much stretched out before him—Cavanaugh land. And he was a Cavanaugh.

His phone buzzed and he glanced down at the screen.

Cowboy? You still there?

Someone passed away tonight.

Oh. I'm so sorry. Someone close to you?

The opposite. A bad man. Bastard got what he deserved.

Then why do you seem so sad? If this piece of shit got what he deserved?

Blue hesitated. It wasn't like Cowgirl to cuss or sound so caustic in her texts. But then again, he knew he sounded down in the mouth. Maybe she was just giving him support. He texted her back.

Forget about him. It's you and me that matters. I want you. I want to know you,

Cowgirl. Know your real name. See your
face. Touch you. Kiss you.

I want that too.

His heart seized, longing barreling through
him. He needed this now. Her. This one person he
trusted. He needed to have her in front of him. See
her in the flesh.

When?

Blue stared at the screen, waiting. She wanted
this too. Since they'd started talking, she'd made
it very clear how she felt about him. It was time.
Enough of the games. It wasn't fun and mysteri-
ous anymore.

He waited. The minutes ticked by. But he got no
reply.

Nineteen

"I'm not kidding when I say I'm going to have a heart attack," Grace said, panting and sweaty as they headed into the second mile.

Annoyingly dry, his breathing unlabored, Cole jogged beside her. "No you're not."

"You don't know my medical history, Cole!"

"True, but I've seen you engage in other forms of exercise where heavy breathing is involved. You sailed right through it. I'm thinking it's not the exercise, but the type of exercise. Or even better, the reward."

She faux glared at him. "Can I once again say you have a perverted mind?"

"I don't know," he said on a grin. "Can you say it again?"

She tossed him a snarl. "I hate you."

He grinned back. "No, you don't."

"I want to beat you with a stick."

"Mmmm . . . I might let you."

"Perverted!" she cried out just as they hit Main Street. "Oh my God." Grace stopped, folded over, and just tried to pull in air and not feel like she might explode from the inside out. Oh, stopping was so good. Fantastic. The best ever.

She felt Cole's hand on her back. "You didn't have to do this."

"You asked me to go jogging with you," she managed to get out.

"You could've said no."

She glanced up. "And let you think I'm an out-of-shape wimp? Absolutely not. Better to show you that firsthand." She squinted at him through her sweat haze. "How are you so . . . ?"

"What?"

Gorgeous. Sexy. Irresistible. The no-shirt policy was really growing on her. And the white-and-gray shorts that hung on his hip bones showed off both his hard abs and his muscular legs, which incidentally possessed just the right amount of hair. If she was not having a heart attack that very second, she'd jump him. Or try to. He was so damn disciplined about the no-sex-before-a-fight thing, though.

The night before, he'd slept beside her and woken up with a hard-on. She'd felt it against her lower back and tried to coax him to use it by moving her butt around. He'd gotten out of the bed and into the shower so fast Grace believed he might be part jackrabbit.

"Dry," she finally spat out. "How are you so damn dry and not out of breath?"

He laughed. Silently saying, *You know I do this for a living, right? Test the limits of my body on a daily basis?* But aloud, he asked, "What are you doing later? After you recover, of course? Want to have a late lunch, early dinner? With me?"

She straightened, groaned at the resistance of her muscles to anything more. Dinner. Food. Vomiting was not out of the question right now. "Let's walk. Slowly." She started forward. "Need to walk."

He followed her. "You want me to carry you, honey?" The damn grin was in his voice now.

"You're very kind. But I just couldn't bear that."

"I've done it before. Enjoyed it too."

"I was not sweat soaked and stinking to high heaven at the time."

"You think that's a turnoff?"

Her head came around and she stared at him. His black eyes glowed with health and wickedness. She shook her head, even managed a smile. The guy could make her grin through tears and near total collapse.

They moved down the street at a snail's pace and into the midmorning bustle of River Black, past the hotel.

"I'm going to be gone all tomorrow," Cole said, picking up the conversation. "Back to Austin, and then the fight's the day after. I want to see you before I go."

She wanted that too. "I'd like that, but I'm going to Palmer's funeral."

It was as if all the air was suddenly sucked from the town. Cole stopped and faced her, all good humor gone. "You're really going to that freak show?"

His quick ire caught her off guard. "He was my father's best friend, Cole—"

"Okay, but what does that have to do with you?"

"I'm taking my dad," she informed him.

His brows knit together. "Do you really think that's a good idea? Putting your dad through that?"

"He doesn't know what Caleb did," she said, feeling a blanket of unease move over her. "This is a connection to the life he had. Maybe it'll bring something back." Her gaze faltered. "Maybe it'll bring me back."

He sighed, glanced past her. "Yeah, I get that. And if he remembers Palmer and you, maybe he'll remember something about Cass."

Grace understood his unwavering need to get answers. And when she felt the hurt rise up within her, she tamped it right back down. They both deserved their heart's desire. She just prayed Cole's wouldn't come at the price of her father.

"You want to go together?" she asked him.

His whole face warmed to her. "You sure?"

"Yeah." She sounded a little uneasy. Maybe she felt that way too.

Cole reached out and touched her shoulder. "I won't push him, Grace."

Her eyes found his and she nodded. She hadn't expected that from her fighter. She knew what was at stake for him. And she respected it. But giving her and her dad the night . . . it meant the world. It meant he was capable of feeling deeply.

There was a moment of awkwardness between them. Cole unsure what to say. Grace nervous about what the night might bring. Then Cole said, "I'm going to keep going." He gave her a soft smile. "I have another eight miles to get in."

She rolled her eyes. *Show-off*. Then managed a smile. "I'm limping off to the clinic, then. I have a full day of patients."

"You sure you don't want me to carry you there?" he asked, his eyes bright with humor.

"You better get out of here before I take you up on that."

He laughed. "I'll text you."

"Okay."

He started away, but about ten feet out he turned and came back. Before Grace could say a word, he took her face in his hands and kissed her. Not a hungry kiss, but soft and meaningful.

When he pulled back, his eyes roamed over her face. "Have a good day, Doc." Then he grinned. "I like saying that."

She watched him go, so strong, moving so much faster than he had with her by his side. He was glorious.

I like saying that, he'd said.

I like hearing it, Grace thought as she turned toward the clinic and propelled herself and her aching muscles forward.

There was nothing Cole wanted to do less than sit on a hard bench in that damn church and listen to a man he despised get eulogized by a man who clearly wanted to claim the woman he was with.

But he'd done it. Along with the whole town, who—despite Palmer's despicable actions—had come together to send him off.

Or down, depending on what you believed.

Deacon and Mac had come too, and of course Grace and her father. Cole had made sure his brother knew that questions were off-limits tonight. Out of respect and care for Grace.

After the church service, they'd traveled over to the Shurbots' place for the reception. There was no way Cole was going to Caleb Palmer's grave site. The man didn't deserve anyone's respect, much less Cole's.

"You want something?" Deacon asked, coming up beside him with a paper plate.

They were standing near the grill in Carl Shurbot's backyard with about fifty others. Townsfolk who had once been friends with Caleb Palmer. Thought him a decent man. It was hard to accept the idea that one of their own could be a monster who hurt women.

"Hamburger without the bun or whatever it is you eat?" His brother grinned.

"Don't pick on him, Deacon," Mac cut in, looking all cleaned up in a navy dress and heels. "Cole loves a good bun. Don't you, Cole?"

"You two are really hilarious. And this is the perfect place to crack jokes, by the way."

"Oh, come on, little brother," Deacon said, giving Harry Appleton a wave as he passed by. "This is as much a celebration of life as it is a celebration of death."

"You're going to hell, Deac. You know that, right?"

"I do. And I feel right comforted that you'll be there alongside me."

Mac slipped her arm through Deacon's. "Well, I'm starving. Burger with the bun, please."

"Coming right up, darlin'," Deacon said, leading her away from Cole and toward the grill.

Cole took the opportunity to check on Grace. She was over at a long table with Ben Shiver, Mrs. Remus, and her dad, who seemed remarkably lucid tonight. Cole had driven them both to the church, and the man had spent much of the time talking about movie night at the senior care center. Cole had wanted to test the waters with a little chat about the past, but he'd promised Grace.

She looked up and spotted him watching her. She waved and he nodded. He was trying to give her some space, let her spend time with her dad.

After all, he was learning nothing of value here. He hadn't heard one thing about Palmer or the past that had to do with Cass. It was as if she hadn't been known to the man's circle at all.

Maybe it was just as well. The fight was just two days away. He could use his anger, his frustration, to bring Fontana to his knees. It was what he'd always relied on. Fire in his belly.

"Someone's looking at you." Deacon was by his side, full plate. "Like they're interested, if you know what I mean."

Cole's eyes searched out Grace again. But she wasn't looking at him. His gut tightened. When had the Rev sat down beside her? he wondered irritably. Chatting her up, laying that *I'm a good guy who wants a future here in River Black, kids and white fences and housecoats and boring sex and blah blah fucking blah* on her.

He was about to head their way when Deacon knocked his chin in a different direction. "Not her," he said. "Over by the garden beds."

The Shurbot place was pretty extensive and well appointed for a small ranch property. Past the small barn was a row of garden beds, full to bursting with greens and sunflowers.

"I don't see any girl looking my way," Cole said.

"Didn't say it was a girl."

Cole was about to deck the man for jerking his chain when he realized Deacon was right. There was a man staring at him.

"Who is that?" Cole asked.

Deacon shook his head. "Never seen him before. But he seems real interested in you."

Maybe the guy had seen one of his fights. Cole tried to place him. He was busy running his eyes up and down Cole's body the same way Grace did. But it didn't feel the least bit romantic. More like a cop checking out a suspect. But a confused, freaked-out sort of cop.

"Hey, Carl," Deacon called to the older man working the grill. "You know who that is? Over near your greens?"

Stepping away from the barbeque, Carl squinted. "Oh, I believe that's Caleb's nephew. I think his name is Billy Felthouse. Lives in California."

"A relative," Deacon murmured to Cole. "He seems pretty into you. But I bet you don't want to date into that family."

"What was that, boys?" Carl asked, picking up his tongs once again.

"Nothing, Carl," Cole said, giving Deacon the stink eye. "Just remarking on how we'd never seen the guy before."

"No, you wouldn't have. When he stayed here, he didn't go to school or nothing. And he was only around a short time. 'Bout a dozen years ago, I think it was. Something happened to his daddy and he was up and gone from here before his boots had time to settle in the River Black dirt."

The words went into Cole's brain, setting off a

roar so startling he lost his breath for a second. He glanced over at Deac. Oh yeah, he'd heard it too.

Neither one of them said a word as they made their way over to the garden beds. Cole's heart was hammering in his chest. Painful-like. For the first time in a long time, he felt the rustle of fear move through him.

Standing close to six feet with light brown hair and eyes, the man looked both amazed and trepidatious as Cole and Deacon approached.

"Evenin'," Deacon said, his voice reed thin.

The man nodded. "Hi there." His accent was strange. West Coast. He turned to Cole, his gaze wide and intrigued. "Do I know you?"

"You're looking at me like you do," Cole said. He didn't know how to feel. Didn't know what he wanted to happen. But he knew whatever it was, it was coming his way full force.

"It's just . . ." The man shook his head. "You look like someone. Someone I used to know. It's just kind of shocking."

"A girl?" Cole asked tightly.

Warm recognition lit the man's eyes. "Yes."

Deacon blew out a breath. And Cole knew without a shadow of a doubt that the man standing before him was the boy known as Sweet.

Twenty

Grace was unsure if she belonged. Not seated beside Cole, but at this table, hearing this discussion.

A little over an hour before, Cole had come up to her at Caleb's reception, his face twisted into a mask of pain, shock, anger, hope, and fear. He'd told her he'd needed to go, that something had come up that trumped everything. He'd told her that Carl Shurbot or Eli Appleton would take her and her father home—or if she was more comfortable, she could take his truck. He'd get a ride with Deacon.

For one brief moment, she'd stared at him. Wanting to ask, wanting him to tell her what was happening. But his eyes spoke volumes about the torment going on inside his soul, so she'd enlisted the help of one of her father's closest friends, Cory Craft, to take him back to the care center, and she'd gone with Cole.

The ride in his truck had been a silent affair. She didn't ask him what was happening or where they were going. Just put her hand over his as he palmed the gearshift and held on tight. The contact seemed to make him breathe easier. Even when he pulled into the driveway of the Triple C. Even when they went inside, sat down together at the large table in the Cavanaugh family's kitchen.

The man they'd all come here to see and talk to was seated between Deacon and James, across from Cole and her. He wore relaxed clothing, had a healthy tan, and longish sun-touched hair. He appeared nervous but resolute, as if glad this time had come.

"I knew she had brothers," Billy Felthouse said, looking from one to the other. "Knew you were protective, as you should be. But we both kept our families out of it."

Deacon didn't like that at all. He glared at the man but didn't interrupt him. Each of the Cavanaugh brothers had come there to finally hear and see and know a piece of the puzzle. And nothing—not even their brotherly protectiveness—was going to get in the way of that.

"It started innocent and ended innocent, I promise you." A faint smile touched his lips. "She was a life force, that one. Felt it from the moment we met in the candy aisle of the dime store. I was buying SweeTarts—"

"That's where the name came from," Mac interrupted passionately, looking from the man to Deacon. "I thought it was because she thought you were so sweet."

He nodded. "I was Sweet and she was Tarts. And boy did that fit her." He laughed. "She was a tough, bright, spunky girl."

Cole's hand tightened around Grace's. It felt hot and a little sweaty, and she knew this had to be insanely painful for him. Hearing about his twin in the past tense. But maybe, just maybe, it would give him some sense of peace.

"Did you know she'd been taken?" Deacon asked, his tone unemotional, as if he was talking to a work colleague instead of the man who'd been so close to their sister.

Billy shook his head. "Like I told you back at Carl's place, I was gone by then. Left for California on the eleventh of May. I remember because it was her birthday the next day and I didn't get a chance to say good-bye. I thought I'd be able to contact her after things got settled. But my dad was really sick, and we were all consumed with it. It's why I came to River Black and stayed with my uncle Caleb in the first place, to give my mom a break—me a break." His eyes clouded. "Cass was taken on the fifteenth. My dad died two days before that. We were planning his funeral. I haven't been back here until now." He exhaled heavily. "When I heard Cass was . . . when she passed away, I wanted to reach out, but it didn't feel right, and I was going through so much with my own dad's death and my mother's grief, and just trying to hold on emotionally and every other way. I was a mess."

His face a mask of pain, James asked through gritted teeth, "You didn't think to get in touch with her family?"

"I didn't honestly think I had anything to offer. I'd been gone for months by the time I heard what had happened. And no one tried to contact me or my mother. So I thought it was best. I didn't want to stir up trouble."

The men just glared at him. Mac too. And Elena moved silently around them with coffee, tea, and some sandwiches, which remained untouched.

"Were you ashamed of your relationship with Cass?" Cole asked between tightly clenched teeth. "Is that why you kept it a secret?"

"No." The man looked appalled at the thought. "Granted, I was a little older than her—"

"Too old," Deacon ground out.

The man nodded. "Four years. I was barely seventeen. Maybe that wasn't right. But I don't think that's why we kept things to ourselves. For me anyway, I didn't want anything to spoil it. I was having a hard time, and I found such peace and happiness when I was around her. Romance was such a small part. We kissed a couple of times.

No . . . it was a friendship. She was there for me when I didn't feel like I had anyone." He swallowed hard, his jaw clenching. "I wish I had been there for her."

Silence fell around the table as each brother took that in. And, Grace believed, wished the very same thing. No doubt, had been wishing it for a long time.

"She had a diary," Mac said softly, looking so vulnerable and sad Grace wanted to reach across the table and hug her. "Did you know about it?"

Billy shook his head. "Not surprised, though." His smile was gentle. "She liked to talk and work things out. She reminds me of my daughter."

"You have a family?" Grace asked, then pulled herself back. She didn't want to butt in where she didn't belong.

He took out his phone, set it on the table. "That's my wife, Darcy. And my little girl, Hannah. She's two going on twenty."

He turned it around so everyone could take a look at the screen. Grace only glanced at it. She was too busy looking at the brothers. Misery floated like storm clouds behind each set of eyes. They seemed deflated, not knowing what to say or where to go from here. After years of wondering, they now finally had some answers. Yes, he existed. No, he claimed, he had nothing to do with her death. They'd be sure to see that his story checked out. Hell, Deacon probably already had his lead detective on it. But Cole knew that a guilty man wouldn't be sitting here in the kitchen of the Triple C ranch. He'd have run the second he saw Cole or Deacon or James. Probably wouldn't have come to River Black at all. Funeral or no funeral.

"Her death is still unsolved," James said, heat-laced frustration in his tone. "I'm starting to think we'll never know the truth."

Billy was grave. "I'm so sorry. For all of you. You have no idea how sorry. If I can help in any way . . ."

"Do you remember anything from back then?" Deacon pushed, though he seemed as emotionally wrecked and exhausted as the rest. "Anyone who may have disliked Cass?"

"I can't imagine it," Billy said. "And I didn't see it. She was great to everybody, treated everybody with a smile. And they loved her for it."

Grace turned to Cole. He was nodding. Probably not even aware of it. She squeezed his hand.

"Anyone that she talked about . . . being scared of?" Deacon continued. "Or who worried her?"

That made Billy pause. "Well, she did think— we both thought—we were being followed at one point."

"Followed," Cole repeated.

Deacon turned to Mac. "She ever say anything about that to you?"

Mac shook her head and her eyes filled with tears. No doubt she was wondering why her best friend hadn't shared any of this with her.

"It bothered her a lot," Billy continued. "She was scared it was one of you. Or her parents. That you'd found us out."

Cole's eyes were pinned to the man. "Do you know who it was?"

He nodded, sniffed. "It was nothing. Turned out to be my crazy cousin."

"Natalie?" Mac said.

"I'm sure you're aware she has some issues . . . I'm embarrassed to say it, but she had a crush on me." He shook his head. "Would follow us around."

Cole turned to Grace. *The photographs in the newspaper,* his eyes said. She nodded.

"Caleb talked to her," Billy continued. "Helped her understand how inappropriate that was, and she stopped. Even became friends with Cass. Which was good."

"Caleb," James ground out. "Did you know your uncle tried to kill my fiancée?"

Billy looked instantly horrified. "I knew he was in jail for something, but my side of the family hasn't been close with theirs in years. I only came as a courtesy. He took me in all those years ago when my mom was caring for my dad and I needed . . . Christ, I thought I owed him that." He looked at Sheridan. "I'm so sorry."

She smiled. "It's okay. Thank you."

"He said something to me," James continued, his ocean-blue eyes fierce with hatred. "After I pulled him off Sheridan at Mac and Deacon's wedding. He claimed to know who took Cass, who killed her."

Billy's eyes widened. "You don't think that's true? You don't think he—"

"Oh hell, I wish that were the case," James said. "But it turns out your uncle had an alibi that night, so no. He was boasting that he knew who it was, though."

"He might've just been trying to get you off him, James," Cole said tightly. "I know how men get when your hands are wrapped around their neck. They'll say whatever they have to to get away."

"I know you believe that," James ground out, tossing Cole a dark glare. "Not sure I do."

"Poor Natalie," Mac said, shaking her head. "Caleb Palmer for a father, and not being able to get back to the bakery, the one thing she loves. The one thing that gave her the attention she so obviously craved."

Billy nodded. "She was always looking for attention and affection. Being an only child was hard on her. We used to have great fun when we were younger. When our families were closer, and we came out here sometimes. We were Cowgirl and Cowboy, riding the range. She always wanted to live on a ranch."

"What did you say?" a male voice cut in.

Billy glanced over to the stove. Blue was leaning against the counter. Though he wanted to hear what was going on, clearly he had an aversion to sitting with the Cavanaughs. Maybe it was because they had yet to accept him as such.

"She always wanted to live on a ranch," Billy repeated. "She coveted that life. Growing up here and having a house in town was—"

"No," Blue interrupted fiercely. "What you called each other."

"Oh. Cowboy and Cowgirl?"

The man's face turned ashen.

"Blue?" Mac said. "What's wrong?"

Two fiery sapphire eyes rested on her; then he shook his head and turned away, left the kitchen. Mac pushed back her chair and followed him. Elena too, setting down the coffeepot on the counter as she went.

"Did I say something?" Billy asked.

"Seems we're all hearing shocking things today," Deacon said. He stood up and released a breath. "Why don't I take you back to your hotel? I think we all need to sit with this for a while. I'll be checking things out. Making sure what you say is truth."

"Of course," Billy said, coming to his feet. "I'll give you all my contact information. Feel free to call or e-mail me with any questions." He looked at both Cole and James. "And again, I'm so sorry for your loss."

Anger threatened to pierce Blue's calm, cold exterior as he stood on the front porch and dealt with the problem at hand.

"Blue, please." His mother was hovering just inside the door, wanting to step out onto the porch and join her son and Mac, but hesitating as she felt the frost coming from his direction. "Whatever it is, whatever happened in there, I want to help you."

Something pinged in his chest as he looked at the woman who'd raised him, loved him. And lied to him. "I don't want your help."

"Blue," Mac started, warning lacing her tone.

"What?" he snapped, glancing her way.

"Ease up." She gave him a shocked look. She'd never seen him this way. She had better get used to it.

"No, it's fine, Mackenzie," Elena said, trying to keep her voice light. "I'm not going to push him. But I'm here for you, Blue." She backed up a few steps. "And I hope someday you can forgive me."

"Elena, wait," Mac called after her. But the woman was gone, closing the front door behind her. She turned to Blue. "Unbelievable."

"I agree," he said, walking over to the railing. "She won't give up."

"Not her, you jerkoff. You!" She followed him. Stood beside him. Stared at him while he looked out at the land beyond. It was vast and dark, the trees and outbuildings just shapes in the distance.

."I love you like a brother, Blue," she said. "But if you don't stop treating her like shit, I'm going to pound your ass into the ground."

There was a time when this worked. This banter back and forth. She as the big sister. He the hired hand and best friend who took any and all advice she dished out. But not anymore.

He looked over at her. "I love you too, Mac. But you don't get to decide how I feel anymore."

She looked shocked. "I'm not trying to."

"Yeah, you are," he countered. "And it's gotten worse ever since Everett passed and the land was split four ways. You want what you want and that's fine. But no one gets to tell me how to react to what's happened here. How to feel. What to do. What's right. None of it."

She stared at him hard, pointed at the front door. "What happened in there? Just now? Because I know this isn't all about my advice and meddling ways."

A quick smile touched his lips. "What happened was that I realized for the first time that I have no one I can trust."

Mac looked as if he'd just slapped her across the face. Too bad Blue didn't much give a damn tonight.   •

"Go back in there," he said. "To your husband."

Tears pricked her eyes. "I don't know who you are."

"I'm a Cavanaugh," he said evenly. "And the man who is soon to be your boss."

Then he turned away and headed down the porch steps.

Twenty-one

Seconds after they were out of the car, Cole had Grace in his arms. His mouth crushed over hers in a sweeping, hungry kiss that made her gasp. His mind went blank—white-page, gray-screen blank— and he took her up the porch steps with him. Her purse fell to the ground and he slid the sweater from her shoulders.

She moaned against him, and for a second their teeth clashed. Then they were at it again. He knew she could feel his cock against her stomach, knew she wanted it. And he wanted to give it to her.

Blank screen.

Just feel. She's all you want. All you need right now.

Somehow she got the door open and they stumbled inside. His hand slipped under her silk top and raked up her hot skin until he found her breast. He cupped her, squeezed her, then tucked his fingers inside her bra and played with her nipple.

"Oh God," she rasped between kisses. "Cole . . ."

He kicked the door shut with his boot and pressed her back against it, his free hand pinning hers above her head. "I need you," he said, rolling her nipple between her thumb and forefinger. "Shit, I never thought I'd say those words."

"You have me," she whispered. "And you know, I'll be there for the fight."

"That's not what I mean," he rasped, then leaned in and kissed her neck so hard she gasped and tried to get free. "I need you. I need all of you." His mouth was on her collarbone. Her skin was so soft. "Tell me you want this. You want me." He couldn't believe he was saying it—asking for it—but he was.

"I want you more than anything," she said breathlessly.

"Then let me take you to bed. Forget about everything that's happened, everything that's coming. Block out the whole goddamned world with me."

She stilled beneath him.

"Come on, Doc. Please."

"No." The word came out in a rush of air.

Cole lifted his head and took her mouth again. This time in a gentle, urging kiss.

"No, Cole." This time, she strained against him, and when he released her she headed straight for the couch. Belle was sprawled out on two of the cushions, fast asleep.

Eyes wide, body on fire, he turned to look at her. "Grace, you just said—"

Her cheeks were flushed. "We're talking about you and me making love for the first time. I want that. I want all of you."

"This is all of me," he countered, raising his arms in surrender.

She shook her head. "It's a part of you. The part that wants to escape. The part that doesn't want to deal with what he heard tonight." She covered her mouth with her hand, looking utterly bereft. "If we do this . . . if we're together tonight . . . and you lose to Fontana, are you going to blame me? Are you going to blame yourself?"

Cole froze. "Where is this coming from?"

"I know you've existed, even found success, in a world where you're responsible for Cass's abduction. And I wonder if you're worried that will all go away if the truth is revealed."

"I want the truth," Cole returned hotly. "I want to know what happened to her."

"Of course you do. I don't mean it like that. But as you said, you rely on not knowing. You need the fear and anger—"

"Fine," he cut in. "I use the anger."

"No, you use the guilt."

Pain cut into him. He'd thought he was impervious to it. But that's what happens when you let in some light. You can't exist in the gray anymore. "Don't do this, Grace. Not tonight."

"I understand why you fought, Cole. Why you continue to fight. But what happens when the battle's over? Will this be your life even when you know the truth?"

"The battle will never be over," he told her, turning away.

"Why?"

He turned back sharply. "Because I will always be to blame for Cass being taken!"

"That's just not true."

"Right," he said bitterly. "There are others who bear some responsibility. Like your fucking father. If he'd done his job instead of covering shit up to protect his psychopathic friend, maybe none of this would ever have happened. Maybe me and Deac and James would be normal, and not feel like throwing the hell up every time we enter that house." He broke off with a strangled cry. "Fuck!"

Grace was shaking as she came to her feet. "Oh, Cole." She breathed, coming toward him. But he stopped her with a look.

"No. I don't want your pity," he ground out. "I don't want anything. I'm going home."

"And where is that?" she asked gently. "Not here. The hotel in Austin where you keep your stuff? The Triple C?"

"Why are you doing this?" he demanded, his insides quaking. "Why are you breaking me down?"

"Because I'm not into you anymore, Cole." She gave a small shrug. "I think I'm falling in love with you. And I need to know where your head is at. You need to know where your head is at."

Her words tore through him like a hundred silver bullets. Love. *Love?* Was she actually saying . . . ? He couldn't . . . Fuck . . .

"What I need is to go," he mumbled, raking a hand through his hair.

"Where?" she demanded.

He turned around and headed for the front door. "Doesn't matter."

Blank screen.

White noise.

"Wait!" she called after him from the porch. "Cole, don't leave."

But he was already in his truck, gunning the engine, cranking the music. Without looking at her, he sped off. It was only when he was nearing Deac's place that he glanced down at his cell phone. It was facing up on the passenger seat and the screen glowed in the dark light of the truck's cabin.

Just let me know you're safe. —G

*   *   *

Grace turned *Project Runway* off and went to sit down at the small table near the window.

"That's one of my shows," her father complained.

"I know, Dad." She waited a second or two. Waited to see if he'd know her today. The day before, at Mr. Palmer's funeral, her father had been fairly present. He'd known who she was, and a few others he'd been close to over the years. But strangely, he'd talked about Caleb as though the man was still alive.

She was hoping he'd do the same today.

"Caleb Palmer is a good friend to you, I know," she started, opening a box of juice and taking a sip.

"The best," her dad confirmed with an affectionate nod.

"How'd you two meet?"

The slightly lost look her father had sported for the past several months was replaced by a wide, lucid grin. "We fell for the same girl."

She sat forward in her chair. "Really?"

"In grade school. Caleb and I would fight about everything. We was damn competitive. But he knew how much I loved Millie, so he backed off."

Her heart squeezed. "Millie?"

"My wife. Turned out as it should, though, because Millie never cared much for Caleb anyway."

Grace felt tears at the back of her throat at the mention of her mother, but she pushed on. "Oh? Why's that?"

He looked down at his hands, shook his head. "She never gave me a reason when we were kids. But later, she just said he wasn't her type of man.

Made her nervous instead of calm. I made her feel calm."

Grace wondered if her mom had sensed something wasn't right with Mr. Palmer. Wondered if there had ever been an issue with him that Millie hadn't disclosed because he and her husband were so close.

"You said once you felt you owed him," Grace said gently. "What did you mean by that?"

"Well, he gave me my Millie, of course." He bobbed his head from side to side. "So I made sure he didn't lose his family."

Grace's heart started to beat wildly in her chest. "Was he in danger of losing his family?"

Her father didn't say anything.

"How did you make sure he didn't lose them, Dad?" she pressed. "Dad?"

"I want to watch my show now."

"Dad, please," she begged. "I'll turn your show on, but first you've got to tell me."

"Why do you keep calling me that? I didn't have any children." His eyes narrowed. "Who are you? Do we work together?"

For a split second Grace contemplated saying yes, telling him she was from the sheriff's office and she wanted information on Cass Cavanaugh and Caleb Palmer. She wanted so desperately to give Cole something. Anything. Even at the cost of her own hopes and prayers regarding her father's involvement.

She got up and turned the television back on. But instead of returning to her chair, she sat on the edge of her father's bed and watched as Heidi Klum laid out the rules for the next challenge. Tears rolled down her face. She felt she'd failed. She felt alone. And she knew that she'd pushed Cole too far. But she'd had to. He'd needed to hear it. How long was long enough to punish one's self?

She hadn't heard from him all day. And last night, he hadn't texted her to tell her he was home safe. She knew he was only because she'd called Mac. Cole had left for Austin last night on Deacon's helicopter, the woman had told her.

He was probably done with her. Didn't want her anywhere near the fight. In his mind, she'd tried to break him down instead of support him. And maybe that was true. But her breaking him down was only so he could start to rebuild his life.

Happy.

With her.

But she'd gone about it the wrong way. At the wrong time. She stared up at the screen. For a healer of animals, she sure knew how to destroy their human counterparts.

Twenty-two

Cole shifted from foot to foot inside the small room off the main event area, keeping warm and stretching out his neck. He was tense. But that was nothing new. Every fight he'd ever had, from the first to tonight, had started with a restless, impatient feeling. He wanted to draw blood. He wanted to win.

"You ready? You look ready."

He glanced over his shoulder, spotted Matty in the doorway. "She out there?"

"Doesn't matter."

He turned away, inhaled sharp and quick. Antiseptic and massage oil. *Doesn't matter.* Was the man serious? 'Course it mattered, damn it. Grace wasn't there. They'd fought and he'd walked out and she'd texted him and he hadn't answered because he was a scared bastard.

He raked his hands through his nearly shaved skull. He felt like his insides were going to explode. What was wrong with him that he didn't pick up the phone and call her? Text her? Something that indicated he still wanted her here.

That he needed her.

And not because he couldn't win without her. Oh, he was going to win. And big. But because he was more than just "into" her too, and when she'd said all that true shit to him he'd felt exposed and vulnerable.

"Your brothers are out there," Matty said. "Their girls too. Your infatuated doctor from Dallas."

He nodded. He'd screwed up with Grace. Drew back and got defensive instead of leaning on her and taking what he wanted, what she was offering. So maybe she wasn't at this fight. He'd make sure she was at the next.

He followed Matty out the door and down the hall, adrenaline kicking his heart rate, priming his muscles. He saw the lights up ahead, flickering hot and electric beneath the curtain. As he'd done a hundred times, he strode through the chute—it's what they called the two metal barriers that separated the fighters from the crowd.

Cole knew the crowd was mammoth and running red hot for a good match and a lot of spilled blood. Tickets had been sold out for months. Fred Omega Fontana and Cole the Cobra Cavanaugh: two underground fighters meeting in a legit match for the first time.

He bumped fists with his crew, put in his mouth guard, and checked the tape on his hands. The rest was all him. Bare feet, bare chest, no gloves, and all ready. The events of the last few days had worn him down, threatened his focus and his heart. But he wasn't going to allow his emotions to penetrate his armor.

He'd worked too hard to build that shit.

The strobe lights blasted blue and silver as he walked through the cage door into the ring. At the same time, Fontana strode in through the opposite side. The man was shorter than Cole by about three inches. But what he lacked in height, he made up for in muscle. Hell, the man looked like an advert for steroids. He grinned at Cole. Cole flipped him off.

The action sent the crowd into ballistic, screaming madness, chanting his name. Granted, he heard it. Oh yeah, he heard it, but he pressed it down. Dull roar, baby. *Nothing but Omega and you. It's time to end this.*

"Ladies and gentlemen," crowed the announcer, who stood in the center of the ring, decked in his penguin suit, microphone in hand. "In the blue corner, weighing in at one hundred and ninety-five pounds, hailing from Cincinnati, Ohio, champion underground fighter Frank Omega Fontana."

The crowd started chanting. *"Fontana. Fontana. Fontana."* But Cole just kept moving, keeping his body warm.

"And in the silver corner," the announcer continued, "weighing in at one hundred eighty pounds,
hailing from right here in Austin, we have Cole the
Cobra Cavanaugh!"

The crowd erupted, and a woman in a bikini
waltzed around the ring with the ROUND ONE card
above her head.

Cole barely noticed. His eyes were pinned on
Fontana. The man was just as ready as he was. He
did a few practice punches, then stalked over to
the left to say something to his trainer. That was
when Cole's eyes caught on something moving
through the crowd.

His heart kicked, and damn if he didn't feel a
surge of sexual heat run through him. Grace.
Looking extraordinarily hot in a white strapless
corset top, black leather miniskirt, bare legs and
heels. He practically drooled. Matty was bringing
her to the front, and when she saw him, she took
out a silver scarf from her purse and wrapped it
around her neck. Damn . . . how had she known?
To wear that? His color.

I'm sorry, he mouthed at her.

It's okay, she mouthed back.

He winked at her. His silver girl. And felt waves
of relief move over him. He was ready now. Going
to give this fight all that he had. Not just for Cass
this time, but for Grace and for himself.

The ref held his arms out to both fighters. "You
ready?" he asked Cole. Cole nodded. He turned to

Fontana. "You?" Fontana grinned. The ref backed up, gave the sign, and the bell clanged.

The animal inside Cole stretched as he moved forward. He and Fontana didn't tap fists like most fighters. They didn't care about that shit.

Fontana lunged, head down, intending to slam him back into the cage, wrestling style. But Cole drove his elbow into the man's shoulder, dropping him to the mat. Only for a second. Before Cole could pin him, Fontana shot back to his feet and followed up with a right and left deep into Cole's gut.

Doubled over, Cole sucked air. What the hell? He wasn't on his game. Where was the anger that fueled him? The guilt that hissed in his veins and kept him alive?

Jesus, he was more pussycat than cobra tonight. And if he didn't pull his head out of his ass, he was going down hard.

The sound of his name snapped his head up.

His gaze collided with his girl. Grace was screaming his name. Not out of fear, but passion, drive. And there it was: his reason. Her. She loved him. Thought him worthy.

Time to show her exactly what he could do.

Shooting upright, Cole shook it off and honed in on Fontana. Keeping the guy's focus on his hands, Cole launched a knee strike.

Shocked, Fontana slammed back onto the mat.

Cole mounted his hips and let the ground-and-pound fly with hammer fists and elbow strikes.

Fontana flipped him off, slamming his knee into Cole's gut. Pain screamed in his abdomen. A second later adrenaline surged within him, tamping down the need to puke.

"Is that your little bitch in the crowd?" Fontana taunted through his mouth guard. "Wearing your colors?"

Cole caught the rage, refusing to respond. Instead, he pulled it in and let it fuel his need to win. *She's watching you. Earn that color she's wearing.*

Earn her motherfucking love.

When he jacked up to his feet, the calculated madness he'd shown once before during training reared its beautiful head once again, and Fred Omega Fontana was basically standing still to him. No sound in his ears, no thoughts in his head, he rushed the other man. Pinning him against the cage, Cole unleashed his fury, his need to win and triumph until the bastard went down with a grunt and a rain shower of blood. And stayed down, forcing the ref to call the fight.

Cole didn't hear the crowd, but he saw it. Mouths open, hands raised. His eyes searched for her. And when he found her, he knew love.

"Hold still," Grace commanded as she stood in front of the sink in Cole's hotel bathroom trying to clean his wounds. He had a mess of them, and was being a big baby.

When the cotton ball touched his temple, Cole drew back with a hiss. "Stings like a son of a bitch."

"'Course it does. It's supposed to." She cupped the back of his head and pulled him to her. "I know this isn't your first time at the rodeo, so to speak."

"No, it's not." He leaned in and stole a kiss. Hungry and filled with lust. Then straightened again. "Fine. Do your worst, Doc."

She shook her head, but her insides were humming with awareness. It felt like ages since he'd kissed her. She knew that wasn't the case, but it felt like it.

This time, when she wet a new cotton ball and dabbed at the three small cuts on his face, he didn't move. Just watched her work. They'd been back at his hotel for only a half hour. After the fight, there had been a media frenzy and several parties to go to, but Cole had wanted only to get her and get out. He wanted to be alone with her. She loved that about him.

"There," she declared, giving a small cut on his neck a final dab. "All done."

He gazed down at her. "I like you nursing me."

"Doctoring you," she corrected.

He grinned. "Right."

"And I like it too." The air between them was hot and electric from battle. "Don't know if I said congratulations." She moved past him and turned on the shower. "You were amazing tonight. Fierce, fast, focused."

"The three *F*'s," he said, then started stripping down.

Grace stared. She'd never seen him naked. She'd imagined it plenty of times. But, boy, did the reality outgun the fantasy. He was muscle head to toe, from calves to thighs, protruding hip bones, washboard abs, and broad, dangerous chest. And he was heavily inked all over. Her eyes moved over his tattoos. She noticed that he had one just under his hip bone on the left side. Looked like numbers maybe. She'd have to get a closer look. Run her tongue over it and see how it tasted. See how everything south of his navel tasted.

"What about the fourth *F*, Doc?" he asked.

She looked up, caught his gaze, and knew her cheeks had turned bright red. "Water's hot. You should get in the shower."

He shook his head real slow. "Not without you."

Heat shuddered through her. "Don't you want a little time? To recover, relax."

He sniffed indignantly. "Fuck no."

She laughed. "Was that the fourth *F*?"

"Kind of." He grinned.

"Oh," she said, suddenly breathless. She couldn't wait for the fourth *F*. Him buried inside her. But she didn't want to push him. He'd been to battle, won the war.

"I'll get in first, Doc," he said, standing before

her, hard everywhere. "But if you're not naked and under the water with me before I finish soaping up, I'm taking you fully dressed."

The dual meaning to his words made her belly clench. She watched him step into the large travertine shower. He had the hottest, tightest ass she'd ever seen. Her hands twitched with just the thought of touching him.

Mine.

All mine.

"Clock's ticking, Doc," he called out, buried under the powerful spray.

Christ, what was she waiting for?

With nervous, excited hands, she removed her clothes, piling them on the sink. Warm, wet air licked over her skin, matching the warmth and growing wetness of her pussy. She'd never wanted anything more, anyone more.

Cole had his back to her when she stepped into the shower, water pummeling his skin, rinsing the body wash off. Her mouth watered as she came up behind him and wrapped her arms around his waist.

"Oh, holy fuck," he growled, pressing into her. He smelled so good. Like cool pine.

"Was that the fourth *F*," she asked, planting a kiss on his shoulder blade.

"Getting closer."

Grinning, she reached down and took his cock in her hand. Pressing herself against him, her breasts to his back, her sex to his incredible backside, she stroked him, slow and easy. He was stunningly hard, like marble, and so warm. The male groan of pleasure that echoed off the walls filled her with such desire and such overwhelming happiness. She was finally able to touch him. Claim him.

Cole reached out and rested his palms on either side of the shower. She trailed kisses up his back, the muscles flexing beneath her lips, his cock growing even harder in her hand. The hot spray was turning the space into a sauna, giving it an even more intimate, closed-off feeling. God, he was so beautiful. A work of art. And he was all hers. She prayed he was all hers.

"My Grace," he uttered, his hips moving now, taking each stroke like a thrust—like he was inside her. "I always want your hands on me."

My Grace. *His* Grace. She smiled through her kisses, through her nips to his skin. She loved that he called her that. Especially now. In their sauna built for two. It meant he not only felt comfortable with her, was turned on by her, but he'd let go of all that had gone down between them recently.

"Oh, Christ," he groaned. "Oh, shit." He sucked in air. "Faster, Doc, please."

Her entire body was humming with a need to please him. As he'd pleased her so many times. She did as he asked, sped up her strokes, tightened her grip, and when she heard him groan and curse, felt his wet heat on her fingers, felt him thrust over and over in her hand, she knew happiness. He'd made her come over and over, and yet could have nothing for himself. Now the battle was over and spoils were ahead.

For a moment, he remained still, body rigid, hands splayed on the tile. Then he turned around and advanced on her like a hungry predator. "Tell me what you want," he growled.

"You," she said wholeheartedly. "You inside me. Finally. Deeply."

"I want that too. Christ. I'm growing hard again just thinking about it. But I need to know what you want outside of this shower, this hotel room."

She hadn't expected that. Not here. Not now. Tonight was supposed to be about pleasure only. Not reality. They would deal with that later.

Much later.

"It doesn't matter," she implored him.

His eyes flashed with possessive fervor. "Matters to me. Shit, it matters to me. I realized it when I saw you walking toward the ring tonight. And I want to give you everything, Grace."

Her heart opened and bled at his words. "You know what I want, Cole." It wasn't the perfect place to have this conversation. In the shower, with the water raining down on them. Soaking their already soaked skin. Or maybe it was.

"A life in River Black," he said.

She nodded. "But I don't expect that from you. I know you. I understand you." Her voice cracked with emotion. "Please, just stop talking now," she implored him, tears threatening, her body on fire. "Unless it's to tell me how deep inside me you plan to go."

His eyes glittered with sudden fire. "Till you can't breathe, Doc."

Oh God. She stared at him, naked, wet, impossibly sexy. She wanted to get down on her knees and make him come again. She wanted to drink him down, then lick her lips and say, *Ahhhhh . . .* But he had other plans. Always had other plans. He took her in his arms, his mouth capturing hers possessively. Heat overtook her senses, both inside and out, and she reveled in his little bites on her lips, his tongue thrusting deep, his possessive kisses.

His body was flush with hers and she felt every hard plane against her soft skin. Felt his cock grow thick between them as his hands raked down her back to cup her ass. God, she was desperate to have him inside her. She squirmed as he kissed her, wrapped her arms around his neck, spread her legs—urging him to take her. But he just laughed and gave her backside a slap.

She groaned. The sting was delicious.

Before she could ask for another, he tore his mouth from hers and dropped to his knees. Just as she'd wanted to do to him. Without any preamble, he spread her lips wide and licked her. Glorious, tantalizing heat enveloped her, and she reached for something, anything to steady herself. As his tongue played with her clit, flicking the tight hot bud, one hand found his head while the other pressed flat against the travertine tile.

Slowly, he eased a finger inside her. She gasped at the sweet invasion and pressed her hips forward. Cole groaned with appreciation, then wrapped his lips around her clit and started to suck gently.

Her body quickened, sending shards of explosive heat through her blood. She was going to come. Her legs were going to give out.

Seconds before she was about to explode, Cole pulled away from her. He grabbed her by the ass, lifted her up with him, and placed her down on his shaft. For a moment, all she could think was how full she felt. How deliciously, impossibly, wonderfully full. So full she could barely breathe. He'd been right.

"This is the fourth *F*, Gracie."

She stared at him, panting and glassy eyed.

"I couldn't stand it when I thought you weren't coming tonight," he uttered through gritted teeth as he started to move inside her. Slow, deep thrusts. "Tell me I didn't royally screw us up."

"No." She breathed. "It was nothing. It's over."

"I want you, Grace." His eyes were intense as he spoke, his nostrils flared. "I want a real life and a real home."

"Oh, Cole—" She breathed, her mind flashing

in and out. She tried to focus. But what he was doing to her . . . Every nerve ending in her body was poised for release.

"Be mine, Grace. Let me move into that house of yours." He grinned all of a sudden, took her back against the cool tile, and gave her three deep thrusts.

Grace gasped. Both in surprise and wonder. It wasn't what she'd expected. It was what she'd prayed for. It was a dream.

"You know I belong there," he growled. "With you and Belle and the rain."

She was nearly there. Her body wasn't hers anymore. It belonged to this man inside her. He owned her now.

"I love you, Grace," he said, battering her with thrust after thrust after thrust until she broke apart under him.

"I love you too," she cried. "So much. Oh, Cole." She came so hard she saw stars against the backs of her eyes. Bucking and moaning, so much emotion bubbling up inside her, she continued to take what he gave until he pulled out of her and came against her belly. Then she sagged against him, clung to him, her head falling to his shoulder.

After moments, minutes . . . hours, she felt him move. Take her with him. She hardly heard him turn off the water, barely registered that he was carrying her out of the shower, drying her off, and bringing her to his bed.

"You okay, darling?" he asked her, laying her down on the cool sheets.

She looked up at him and smiled. He was standing over her, all hard angles and harder muscles . . . like the one already starting to thicken again. Clearly, this man didn't tire.

"Good girl," he said, pulling open the drawer beside his bed and taking out a handful of condoms. "Because this is just the beginning."

A thrill moved through her. "Of what?"

He climbed onto the bed like a hungry panther, his black eyes glittering with promise. "An epic fuckfest."

And with that, he slipped on a condom, pressed her knees back to her shoulders, and sank inside her once again.

Twenty-three

"Can we call you Champ now?" James asked, aiming for the Diet Coke can that sat right in the middle of the row.

Holding his BB gun at his side, Cole eyed his brother. "No—"

"He's the Cobra," Grace jumped in, her green eyes sparkling with happiness. A happiness Cole shared, and never believed he could have. "My cobra," she added, giving him a wink, then promptly raised her gun and hit both the Diet Coke can and the Sprite beside it.

"Damn," James remarked.

"Okay," Mac said on a laugh as she sipped her glass of lemonade from a table beside Cory Craft's lake. "You guys had a good night."

"I'll say," Sheridan put in. She was sitting on the ground petting Belle, who was on her back groaning with ecstasy. "That was some fight. I love MMA."

"You know that's not what I mean, right?" Mac asked her.

"Of course," Sheridan acknowledged. "Just trying to keep things clean. But seriously, we need to go again." She gave Mac a salute with her beer. "Girls' night at the fight."

"You made us proud, little brother," Deacon said, dropping an arm around his wife and picking up a chicken leg. "Cass would've been proud too."

Cole met his brother's gaze and nodded. For the first time since he'd started fighting, he believed that. Maybe he'd begun the whole battle to stave off his guilt and punish a perpetrator he believed would never be caught. But last night hadn't been about hate and guilt. He turned to Grace, his sharpshooter, his friend, his lover, and gave her a kiss on the cheek. Last night had been about desire and skill, and love.

Still irritated from having his can shot out from under him, James muttered, "So you two a thing now or what?"

Sheridan gave him a look. "Private business, right, baby?"

He leaned in and gave her a kiss. "There's no privacy with us Cavanaugh brothers."

"That's unfortunately true," Mac agreed.

Deacon looked nonplussed. "I don't talk about us." He hesitated a moment, then shrugged. "Except to say how beautiful you are and how you make my heart—not to mention other areas of my body—heat up like a Dallas sidewalk in July."

"No, that's not oversharing at all," Mac returned with a laugh. Which was quickly supressed by the hungry kiss Deacon planted on her lips.

"We're a thing," Grace announced, raising her gun. "I'm not afraid to say it. Shout it to the world. Or any wildlife that may be roaming around these parts."

"Like the tomcat," Cole said. "I'm going to catch him for you. Both your strays need a home."

A huge grin spread on Grace's face and she raised her voice and called out, "I'm totally into him."

Cole laughed. "We're more than a thing, Doc. Come on now. We're committed."

Both Deacon and James were paying attention to him now.

"I'm sorry. What?" James said.

"Oh yeah," Cole said, eyeing his sharpshooter. "I'm locking her down before she changes her mind and runs back to the Rev."

Grace giggled, then turned her attention to the five remaining cans on the ledge. The same ledge both she and Cole had come to, at different times of their lives. But had come back here together.

"I was never with the Rev," she said, then punctuated the statement with three shots.

"Nice," Cole said with a whistle. "And you went on dates with the guy. So . . . you know, technically you were with him," he countered.

"A handful of dates," she corrected.

"He kiss you?"

"I'm not answering that."

"Maybe that's best," he muttered, lining up his shot, then taking out the last two cans. "Knocking out a man of the cloth is a sure way to win a one-way ticket to hell."

"I think *man of the cloth* is a Catholic term," Sheridan said, scratching Belle behind the ears.

Everyone laughed. But no one more than Cole and Grace.

"You gonna travel with him, Doc?" Deacon asked before biting into his chicken leg. "Go to all the fights? Front-row seat? Carry the first aid kit?"

"When I can, of course," she said. "Wearing my silver."

"How'd you know about that, by the way?"

"Matty," she told him with a grin. "When I called to make sure I could get in, he told me your color."

Cole nodded. "Sounds like Matty. Interfering bastard. 'Course, you look real pretty in silver, honey."

"Thank you."

"And for the record," he said, turning to face the table where everyone was now sitting and digging in to the feast that Elena had packed, "I'll only be fighting a couple times a year."

The confused expressions came pretty quick.

"Couple times a year?" Deacon repeated.

"That's a light schedule," James remarked. "You usually schedule in one fight a month."

Cole glanced at his girl. She was picking up the cans and placing them back on the ledge. When she looked up at him, he gave her a broad smile. "I'm slowing down," he said. "Need to keep myself here for my woman and my gym."

Everyone fell silent this time. Drinks and chicken legs and watermelon slices were held aloft in suspense.

"What?" James exclaimed. "Gym? What the hell?"

Cole grinned as Grace came walking up to him.

"Gym?" she asked. She shook her head.

"Honey, I don't have a promise ring for you just yet, but I'm hoping you accept this one." He shrugged lightly, his eyes dancing with shocking happiness. "For now." He pulled out a key ring with twin keys on it.

Her eyes lifted to his. "What is this?"

"I bought the old firehouse. I'm turning it into a world-class boxing gym."

Her eyes widened and filled with tears. She threw herself into his arms and hugged him so tight he nearly laughed.

"That firehouse is two blocks from my clinic," she exclaimed.

"Oh, I know. That was one of the key selling points."

When she pulled back to look at him, there was

such love, such promise in her eyes it nearly knocked him out.

"You think Belle would be a good gym dog?" he asked.

Grace looked past him, at the long-eared creature who was no doubt snoring herself into oblivion at Sheridan's feet, and said, "I do."

Cole leaned in to whisper in her ear, "Someday you're going to say those two words for a very different reason."

"Oh, Cole," she whispered. She clung to him, and for a moment no one else existed.

"This sucks," Mac exclaimed, bringing everyone's head around, including Cole's and Grace's.

"What's wrong, darlin'?" Deacon asked her.

"Blue should be here," she said softly. "He's part of this family."

"Call him up," Deacon suggested, handing her his cell phone. "Ask him to come over. I'll bet he knows all about the Crafts' BB gun range."

James laughed at that.

Mac sighed. "He's not answering my calls."

"He'll come around, Mac," Deacon said, hugging his wife tight. "You'll see."

James did the same with Sheridan, pulling her close. And when Grace settled into his side with a contented sigh, Cole saw his future as bright and promising and full of moments just like this one. He was in love with the woman who had healed his brash and oh-so-battered heart.

*   *   *

The sun was a wicked ball of fire in the sky as Blue made his way to the door of Natalie Palmer's duplex. He knew she was home. He'd found out a few things about her, both past and present, since the bomb had detonated the other night.

He knocked on the door. Twice. He wasn't angry, wasn't out for revenge. In fact, he felt oddly cold. As if he could handle anything that came his way. Maybe that meant he was becoming ruthless. His lips twitched. A true Cavanaugh.

Welcome to the family, son.

The door opened gingerly and Natalie Palmer peeked out.

"Hi there," he said.

If he'd had any question or reservations regarding her guilt, it evaporated when he saw the look of utter panic flash in her eyes.

People were a bitch.

She recovered quickly. Swallowing hard and forcing a smile. "You're Blue Perez, right?"

"It's Cavanaugh now."

"Oh, yes. I think I heard about that." She glanced past him, checking for something. His car? People walking by? "You lost your father a short time ago?"

He nodded. "You too."

The fake smile receded. "Yeah."

He nodded, inhaled sharply, leaned against the door frame. "I'm real sorry about that, Cowgirl."

Her dark eyes flared wide and her skin turned a

sickly white. For months he'd been pouring out his soul, his heart, his guts to a woman he'd thought was falling in love with him. And after he'd found out about his mom and Everett, he'd gone to her. He'd trusted her. Only her.

"Can I come in?" he asked evenly.

"Why?"

He shrugged. "Just to talk. I think it's better that you and I talk instead of me and the sheriff." His brow lifted. "Don't you think?"

Her jaw tightened, twisted, and she stepped back. "Come on in."

Her house was very clean, very neat. Two bedrooms, a bath, and a large kitchen, which she ushered him into the minute he stepped across the threshold.

She motioned for him to sit down on one of the vintage red chairs. "What can I do for you, Mr. Cavanaugh?"

"Please," he said. "Call me Cowboy."

She was prepared for it now. There was no shock or panic. "Why would I do that?"

"Did you know who I was the whole time?" he asked. "Or did you find out partway through?"

"No idea what you're talking about."

"Did you actually like me or was it some kind of prank?"

Her eyes flashed at that. "I have work to do."

He shook his head. "Not yet. Not until we get to the truth. Not until you tell me why you pretended to be . . ." Shit, he couldn't say it. *In love with my sorry, gullible ass.*

The phone rang in the other room.

"You gonna get that?" he asked, brow lifted.

"Don't have to."

"Please. I got nowhere to be."

She threw him a caustic look, then fled the room. Blue stared after her, amazed at how he was taken in so easily. He sat down at the table. Cookbooks were strewn everywhere. Mostly baking. Some fine cake decorating. He opened one, then another. She'd never said a thing about cooking or baking when they'd texted. Not a goddamn thing. Why the hell had she played him? What did she have to gain—

His thoughts stuttered, because inside the third cookbook, a massive tome, tucked into the meringue section, was a smaller book. A diary. He stared at it. He glanced up. He could hear her talking in the next room. His heart started pounding in his chest as he opened to the last page.

Diary of Cassandra Cavanaugh

May 14, 2002

Dear Diary,

Just got home from having breakfast with my family. Mirabelle's French toast is the best. It

*almost made me feel better after missing Sweet
so much. Where is he? I haven't heard from him
since the day before my birthday. I wish he'd
have told me who his people are. Then I could've
gone to them and asked. But he'll be back. He
has to.*

*So anyway, my new friend? The one that was
being a lookout so I didn't get into trouble with
my family? Well, she turned out to be a liar. I
thought I could trust her. I thought she was
helping me. But she's the one who's been
following me and Sweet!! Can you believe that?
She admitted it! First thing tomorrow, I'm going
to tell her to never talk to me again, that Sweet
is my boyfriend, and if she doesn't stop when he
comes back I'm gonna tell everybody how awful
she is.*

*Going to the movies with my brothers now.
Talk to you later,*

Cass

Blue looked up, his heart slamming against his
ribs. Natalie was standing there, staring at him.
Her gaze dropped to the book in his hands.

The diary of Cass Cavanaugh.

"It was you," he said.

Don't miss the next novel in
the Cavanaugh Brothers series
by Laura Wright,

BONDED

On sale from Signet Eclipse in September 2015.

One

Some people would call it a long-held crush, but if you asked Emily Shiver directly what her feelings regarding Blue Perez were, she'd probably say it was more like a long-held . . . appreciation. She didn't do crushes. That was so junior high school. Of course, that might have been when she saw Blue for the first time. He'd just come to town with his mother, moved into the Triple C to take care of the house and of Everett Cavanaugh. The older man was alone. Wife had passed on, all three of his boys gone. From the outside looking in, doom and gloom coated that ranch like thick, hungry fog.

But what did anyone expect, right? They'd lost their girl. Cass. In the most painful way imaginable. Firstly, when her brothers had just wanted to do what every other brother would've wanted to do when they were at a movie theater: watch the movie. Not escort their annoying kid sis to the bathroom. Hell, she could do that on her own—and grab some Skittles on the return trip. But there was no return. She went missing. Christ, the terror that family must have felt. And the horror that followed when her body had turned up in the meadow out past Lake Tonka.

The world as they'd all known it was over. Emily remembered those days well. Seemed like the whole town of River Black was just watching and praying and hoping. Their breath held. But it was no use. No coming back from pain that all-consuming. The Cavanaughs were irrevocably destroyed. Seemed like no light would ever find its way to them. Then in came Elena Perez and her son, Blue. Moved in, cleaned up and out. A hope for comfort and peace, and maybe things returning to some new sense of normal. Which they did. For a while. Until Everett passed . . . and the truth of his affair with Elena, long before she'd moved in to the Triple C, and the child they'd created came to light.

"Emily hon," came a voice near her right shoulder. "That's my Coke you're manhandling there."

The kitchen of the Bull's Eye came into focus like someone fiddling with the lens of a microscope. Emily looked up into the gentle dark eyes of Rae, the Eye's longest-going employee, then back down to their hands wrapped around a large red tumbler filled to the brim with black liquid. She instantly released the glass and stepped back from the soda machine.

"Sorry about that, Rae. My brain isn't working well tonight."

With a soft laugh, the older woman placed the bubbling Coke on her tray. "Well, honey, you only have 'bout fifteen minutes left—ain't that right?"

Emily glanced up at the clock on the wall. Quarter of nine. "Can't come soon enough. Along with my addled brain, my feet are pretty much done."

"Give it a few years and a layer of calluses, honey," Rae said before pulling out and heading back into the dining room.

A few years, Emily thought. She was hoping for one at the most. Just enough time to save up for a mortgage on that abandoned store on Main and Kettler. Nothing wrong with serving up drinks and good food, if that was your choice, but she had a dream of opening her own flower shop that she was looking to fulfill.

After getting herself a large Coke to go with the two whiskeys on her tray, she too headed for the dining room. It was a slow night, and she had only one table. A couple of guys she guessed were traveling through because she'd never seen 'em around River Black before, and one tended to see the same people over and over. They'd ordered food and several rounds of drinks. Easy peasy. She'd serve 'em up and get herself home and to bed. And in that fifteen minutes that remained, she would not—repeat, *would not*—stare in the direction of the bar.

As if the silent promise were really an entice-ment to do just that, Emily's brown eyes—which her father called doe eyes, or can't-say-no-to-my-baby-girl eyes—tracked left. Seated at the bar, his back to her, Stetson riding low, was the very object of her . . . What word had she resorted to again? Oh yeah, *appreciation*. And boy oh boy, could she appreciate him tonight. His long, lean, hard body was showcased in nothing special: standard cow-boy gear, jeans and black T-shirt. But her eyes moved covetously over him anyway, from tanned neck to broad shoulders, trim waist and . . . a denim-clad butt that made her heart kick up and certain unmentionable lady parts quiver.

Sigh. She'd worked at the Bull's Eye for a year and a half now, and the man had maybe been in the place twice. Didn't seem like much of a drinker or a socializer. 'Cept maybe with Mackenzie Byrd. They worked at the Triple C together and seemed like friends. Or had. She hadn't seem them around each other lately. Since Mac had gone and married the el-dest Cavanaugh. Emily wondered what had brought him in tonight. And straight to the bar. Where he'd been tossing back—

"Goddammit, girl!"

Emily whipped around. The man before her—a customer she didn't know—had his hands in the air and was staring down at his crotch. Emily swal-lowed as she saw that the denim was sporting a spattering or two of whiskey. She glanced at her tray and the glass on its side. *That's what staring and dreaming does: pissed-off customer, no tips.*

Quickly, she set the tray down on the empty tabletop behind her and grabbed some napkins. "I am so sorry," she began, holding out the napkins. No way was she trying to clean up his crotch. "Here. Please take these."

The man looked up, venom in his pale brown eyes. "What the fuck are you? Blind? Or just clumsy?"

Perfect. No forgiveness here. "I'm really very sorry. Let me get you another, on the house."

For anyone in River Black, this would've garnered a begrudging smile at the very least. But not our out-of-towner. He wanted blood and humiliation.

"So you can spill that on me too?" he snarled at her. "Pass." He turned to his friend, who looked about as nice and as forgiving as jerkweed number one and uttered, "Should've known. Stopping in these tiny towns, all you get are stupid, clumsy bitches with big racks."

Heat spread through Emily's chest, and she felt her lip curl against her top teeth. Assholes came and went. It was part of the job. Maybe not as much in River Black as in the bigger cities, but it happened. For the most part it was always better to walk away from the table or to let Dean handle it. But Emily had never been able to suffer insults or misogyny well. Shoot, she'd grown up with two brothers. They'd stopped thinking they could get away with shit after the age of five. Jerkweed One and Two were going to learn that hard fact right now.

"I'm sorry, sir," she began, her tone low and cool. "I don't think I caught all of that. I have a big rack and what? What did you call me?"

The friend made a low whistling sound before Jerkweed Number One muttered, "No eyes, but she's sure got ears."

"Sure do," she said. "And they're almost as big as my rack."

Both heads came around. Both sets of eyes widened.

"Look," she said, easing back just a touch, giving them room to drop their crap and act civilized. She wasn't looking to have a problem in the Bull's Eye tonight, and hell, her shift was almost up. "Didn't mean to splatter you with the whiskey. I'm offering to buy you another. On me. Be done with this. What do you say?"

For one brief second, Emily thought the Jerkweeds were going to be human. But then Jerkweed One opened his big mouth again.

"You know, darlin," the man drawled, "a man only likes his women feisty in the bedroom. I think someone should teach you some manners."

She rolled her eyes.

"I'll do it," offered Jerkweed Two. Dark eyes glittered under dark brows.

"Okay," Emily began. "I'll get you the check. Or better yet, leave and I'll take care of it."

Jerkweed One laughed. "She thinks she has a say over what I do, Tim." The man snorted and sat back in his chair. "Big tits and a nice ass only sway a man—"

"Okay over there?" came a male voice behind Emily.

A different kind of heat coursed through her this time. It blanketed her with warmth and familiarity, and she instantly turned to see Blue coming up beside her. Tall, strong and handsome, with eyes so fierce they took her breath away.

"Everything's fine," she told him.

"That's right," Jerkweed Number One chimed in. "Get lost, cowboy."

"I'm not speaking to you," Blue said in a voice so cold, Emily waited for her breath to fog up. "Did you think I was speaking to you?"

The man stared back hard.

"Okay," Emily said. Last thing she wanted was a fight. "It's all good here." She gave Blue an encouraging nod. "Seriously, nothing I haven't seen, dealt with or kicked to the curb before."

"Or got down on yer knees for, right, honey?" Jerkweed Two said with a low chuckle. He turned to his friend, the instigator. "That's how we shut her up, right, Tim? Stick something in her mouth."

Tim grinned. "You bet. While I stick something in her—"

That's as far as Tim got. Before Emily could stop him—not that she wanted to—Blue reached out, grabbed the idiot by the collar, jerked him to his feet and slammed a fist into the man's smug face. The guy went flying back into a chair. In seconds, his friend was up and rounding the table, coming after Blue. But the ranch hand was ready. Emily had never seen anybody work so fast. While Rae and Dean were rushing over to a mumbling Tim, Blue had Jerkweed Two in a chokehold and was dragging his ass across the Bull's Eye and toward the door. Emily stared at the man on the ground, shaking her head. He could've just accepted the drink. *Asswipe.*

Suddenly Tim was being hauled to his feet. It was Blue. Controlled ire sizzled around him. He was a good three inches taller and far broader than the other man, and it was a lot more evident as the guy sagged against him. Blue dragged Tim over to Emily.

"What do you say?" he ground out, shaking Tim a bit. "What do you say to her?"

The man blinked, no doubt trying to get his full range of vision back. He looked at Emily. "Sorry. Ma'am."

"Yeah, sure," she returned. "Just, you know, don't ever come back."

Blue handed the man off to Dean, who escorted him out to his waiting friend. Emily glanced at Rae, who just shrugged. It wasn't as though they hadn't seen this kind of thing before. Rae probably several times. Then Emily looked back at Blue. It was then that she noticed he was bleeding. A small gash on his lip—and his chin was bruised. Must've happened outside with Jerkweed Two. Dammit . . . Last thing she wanted was this man getting hurt. That beautiful face. That hard, sexy jawline . . .

This time when she rolled her eyes it was at herself and internal.

She reached for a napkin. "Your lip . . . let me clean it up for you."

He backed away. "Naw, it's nothing."

She stared at him. "You're bleeding."

He swiped at it with the back of his hand. "All gone."

"Well, that wasn't very sanitary."

His eyes—those unbearably blue eyes—warmed with momentary humor. Then he touched the brim of his hat and turned to head back to the bar.

Emily stared after him. Confused. "Wait." She followed him. "Shit . . . I didn't thank you."

"No need," he said, sliding into his seat once again.

"Maybe not. But I'm going to thank you anyway."

He turned to look at her. "Something tells me you could've taken 'em out yourself."

"What tells you that?"

He ran a hand over his jaw, which was darkening by the minute. "Just a guess."

"Are you in pain?"

"Constantly," he returned before picking up his drink.

"You want something, Em?" Dean asked, sliding back behind the bar. "After dealing with those assholes, I say you're done for the night. But a drink is needed."

"It's on me," Blue said, then tossed back his tequila. "Another if you please. What would you like . . . Em?"

Her heart pinged in her chest. "It's Emily."

"Right." He cocked his head to the side as he studied her. "I've seen you around."

Her heart ceased to ping. *Seen her around.* Which was code for *I barely noticed you. Do you even live in River Black?*

"You like wearing a green hat, right?" he continued. "I remember because I always wondered where you got a green Stetson round here."

Oh. Pinging has returned! A smile touched her mouth. He had noticed her. "It was my grandmother's. Dyed for her special by a Native American friend from school." She turned to a waiting Dean. "Just a Coke for me. Thanks, Dean."

Blue groaned. "Ahhh, now you're gonna make me feel bad. Or worse." Under his breath he uttered, "If that's even possible tonight."

Curiosity coiled within her. Did she ask? Did she wait for him to tell her? Did she ignore it?

Dean set the Coke before her and poured another round of tequila for Blue, which he drained in about five seconds flat, then tapped the bar top to indicate he wanted another.

"Thirsty tonight?" she asked gingerly. She'd worked at the Bull's Eye long enough to know that drinking like he was had nothing to do with relaxing. Dark feelings were running through Blue Perez's blood.

He turned, and his eyes moved over her face. "Yep. Green hat and a ton of strawberry blond curls." He reached out and fingered one of those curls caught up in a ponytail.

Emily shivered.

"Here you are." Dean was filling his glass once again, and this time when Blue took hold, he swung it her way in a quick acknowledgment.

"Sure you don't want something stronger, Miss Emily?"

She sipped her Coke. "I think you're doing fine for the both of us. And you'd better be walking home."

"I got my truck."

She shook her head and, like the meddlesome gal she was, reached over and grabbed his keys off the bar top. Blue's gaze found hers, and under the heat of that electric stare, Emily's breath caught.

She held the keys up. "I'm going to take you home when you've sufficiently drowned yourself."

"Not necessary."

"I say it is."

"You don't want to do that, darlin'. I'm not fit to be around."

It was impossible to miss the heavy, pulsing pain that echoed in his incredible blue eyes. She knew some of what had happened to him in the past couple of months. Finding out his daddy was Everett Cavanaugh. That he had part claim to the Triple C. With a set of three new brothers. But clearly there was more. So much more.

She dropped the keys into her jeans pocket and turned to face her Coke. This wasn't how she'd wanted to meet Blue . . . talk to him . . . under the haze of tequila. But he'd offered up some protection for her tonight, and she was going to do the same.

I'm not going to let you get hurt, Blue Perez Cavanaugh. Any more than you already are.

She tasted like heaven, her mouth so warm and hungry, he fell easily in lust with it. His mind was clouded, unusable. But his limbs, his muscles, his tongue, his dick and his will were all alive with feeling.

She was sitting on top of him. Strawberry blond curls falling down past her shoulders, the tips licking her nipples. His mouth watered. That was what he wanted to be doing. Licking those dark raspberries. Tugging at them. Biting.

If he just knew where he was. What he was . . .

No. He didn't want that.

This was his heaven. In the real world, real life, he didn't get to go to heaven. Only with her.

The angel.

He groaned as her warm, soft fingers glided up and down his shaft. "I need to take you," he uttered. "Be inside you. Can I?"

There was a moment's hesitation as if she was thinking. *Don't think. Don't think. It's bad.*

Painful.

Problematic.

"Blue . . . ," she whispered, her voice a hungry whisper.

Was he Blue? Blue Perez? Blue Cavanaugh? The tequila wasn't talking.

Clasping her soft, small waist in his hands, he lifted her up and placed her down on his shaft.

White, brilliant, healing heat surged into him.

Yes.

This.

Her.

"Wait. We need—"

But his mouth was on hers, and his fingers were playing in her hot, slick sex. And all that remained were the sounds of ecstasy and his cock working inside her. It's the only sound that mattered. Only music that should ever fill his ears.

"Oh, Blue . . . God, yes."

"I need to shut it out, angel," he rasped. "Them, all of them. And her. The pain. Please."

And then he was falling. No. No. Not done. Not over.

Heat and tightness and a rush of moisture fisted around his cock.

Hated this. He wanted more. Her. Only her. She fit him.

Idiot. Fool. No one fits.

Only hurts.

He came in a growl of madness, pumping wildly into her—his hands cupping her breasts, his ears filled with her moans. He should . . . should let her go. Now. But he couldn't. Not until she ran. Or lied. Or deceived. That would be all too soon. This woman was from hell. Had to be. And yet she felt like heaven.

Still inside her, he wrapped his body around her.

She was an angel.

Dark and addicting.

His angel.

Blackness spread through his worried mind, and in seconds, he was gone, asleep. He never felt her disentangle herself from his grasp. Never heard her pull on her clothes or whisper a pained, "Oh God," as she hurried from the bedroom of the Triple C's river cottage.

Also available from
New York Times bestselling author

LAURA WRIGHT

Branded
The Cavanaugh Brothers

When the Cavanaugh brothers return home to River Black, Texas, for their father's funeral, they discover unexpected evidence of the old man's surprising double life—a son named Blue, who wants the Triple C Ranch as much as they do. The eldest son, Deacon, a wealthy businessman, is looking to use his powerful connections to stop Blue at any cost. But he never expected the ranch's forewoman, Mackenzie Byrd, to get in his way...

Mac knows Deacon means to destroy the ranch and therefore destroy her livelihood. But as the two battle for control, their attraction to each other builds. Now Deacon is faced with the choice of a lifetime: Take down the Triple C to feed his need for revenge, or embrace the love of the one person who has broken down every barrier to his heart.

"A sexy hero, a sassy heroine, and a compelling storyline...I loved it!"
—*New York Times* bestselling author Lorelei James

Available wherever books are sold or at
penguin.com

Also available from
New York Times bestselling author

LAURA WRIGHT

Broken
The Cavanaugh Brothers

For years, James Cavanaugh has traveled the world as a horse whisperer, but even the millions he's earned haven't healed the pain he hides behind his stoic exterior. Forced to tackle old demons at the ranch, James throws himself into work to avoid his true feelings. Until he meets a woman who shakes the foundations of his well-built walls...

Sheridan O'Neil's quiet confidence has served her well, except when it comes to romance. But after Sheridan is rescued from a horse stampede by the most beautiful cowboy she's ever met, her vow to keep her heart penned wavers.

"Secrets, sins, and spurs—Laura Wright will brand your heart!"
—*New York Times* bestselling author Skye Jordan

S0570